Evidence of V

Advance Praise

"Written in compelling, creative, and near poetic prose, O'Connor vividly introduces the reader to V—a promising 15-year-old singer in 1930s Minnesota sentenced to a reformatory for sexual delinquency. O'Connor uses a mix of fiction with historical case file information to illustrate the myriad ways such facilities exploited, misunderstood, silenced, and traumatized young women who were deemed insolent, damaged, and mendacious. Kin to *Girl, Interrupted, Evidence of V* gives a keen sense of how we have punished (and continue to punish) girls for non-criminal violations, often in a misguided effort to 'rescue and save.'"

— LISA PASKO, author of *The Female Offender: Girls, Women, and Crime*

"With grace and aplomb, Sheila O'Connor's *Evidence of V: A Novel in Fragments, Facts, and Fictions* shines a bright literary light on a dark page of American history. To every "tuff" girl, to every girl who ran wild or got in trouble, to every girl who had to make her own way or raise herself, and to every adult who ever knew such a girl, O'Connor's new novel is for you. O'Connor tells the story of her grandmother V, institutionalized for her sexuality. When our power is too great, when shaming doesn't work, when they don't know what else to do, they lock us up. V is our grandmother, our auntie, our long-ago sister, and our defiant best friend. V is us."

— MAUREEN GIBBON, author of *Paris Red*

"*Evidence of V* is unlike anything I have ever read. Exhilarating, heart-breaking, and haunting, the experience of V's life and times scintillates and sears long afterward. Part mystery novel, poem cycle, police report, ethnographic study, noir screenplay, historical account, existential spreadsheet, medical report, legal history, hometown newspaper article, meta-feminist account, writer's diary, literary collage, psychological assessment, family memoir, social criticism, and several other forms that are uncategorizable, by the end, the reader realizes, through Sheila O'Connor's masterful artistry, that at the heart of the 'lie' of this fiction, lurk deeper truths—that our ancestors and their traumas can never fully be known to us and each of our family histories is a complicated mix of truth and lore and absence."

— ED BOK LEE, author of *Mitochondrial Night*

A NOVEL IN FRAGMENTS, FACTS, AND FICTIONS

EVIDENCE OF

By SHEILA O'CONNOR

Rose Metal Press

2019

Rose Metal Press, Inc.
P.O. Box 1956, Brookline, MA 02446
rosemetalpress@gmail.com
www.rosemetalpress.com

Library of Congress Cataloging-in-Publication Data

Names: O'Connor, Sheila, author.
Title: Evidence of V : a novel in fragments, facts, and fictions / by
   Sheila O'Connor.
Identifiers: LCCN 2019025830 (print) | LCCN 2019025831 (ebook) | ISBN
   9781941628195 (paperback) | ISBN 9781941628201 (ebook)
Subjects: LCSH: Teenage girls--Fiction. | Juvenile detention
   homes--Fiction. | Exploitation--Fiction. | Family secrets--Fiction. |
   Reformatories for women--United States--Fiction. | Singers--Fiction. |
   Nightclubs--United States--History--20th century--Fiction.
Classification: LCC PS3565.C645 E95 2019 (print) | LCC PS3565.C645
   (ebook) | DDC 813/.54--dc23
LC record available at https://lccn.loc.gov/2019025830
LC ebook record available at https://lccn.loc.gov/2019025831

The author would like to thank the editor of *Slag Glass City*, Volume 3, 2017, wherein earlier versions of some sections of this book have appeared.

Photo and artwork credits, as well as permissions and bibliographical material, can be found on pages 257–264.

Cover and interior design by Heather Butterfield.
Cover image: "Mother and Child at Minnesota Home School for Girls at Sauk Centre." Used with permission of Sauk Centre History Museum and Research Center.

This book is manufactured in the United States of America and printed on acid-free paper.

For my children,
Mikaela and Dylan,

and
for the mothers,
Marilyn, Dorothy, and V,

remarkable spirits, all.

Table of Contents

"And now I don't know
What in all that was real."

—*Czeslaw Milosz, "So Little"*

"One of the main faults of the girls, who are of a healthy lot,
and with few social diseases, is that of lying."

—*"Broken Homes Main Cause of Child Failure,"*
St. Cloud Daily Times and Daily Journal-Press, *May 4, 1937*

[Where to start V's story?
V at fifteen in 1935?
V sentenced until twenty-one, for what?

V the family secret I discovered at sixteen.
My mother's missing mother never mentioned to me once.
Shhh.   The sound of V is silence.

Girl of sealed history like all those other girls.
Sealed; therefore buried.

State documents I now excavate for answers.
An official file of facts that read like fiction.

V a fiction built of fragments, as girls so often are.]

I.

A BOOK OF PSEUDONYMS AND LIES

"First the facts, next the proof of facts, then the consequences of the facts."

—*Henry Clay Trumbull,*
Teaching and Teachers, *1884*

WHO: V, mother of my mother. Absent and erased. V, maternal grandmother. Both missing and maternal?
Mr. C, maternal grandfather?
June, born of V and Mr. C.
June, my mother not maternally inclined.

WHAT: The mystery: My mother's lost beginning. V unknown. A fifteen-year-old girl.
Files unsealed by the county with permission from the court. Buried family facts unearthed.
Making sense of fact with fiction. Always fiction.

WHEN: The Research: 2001 to present day.
The Story: 1935 to ad infinitum.
The length of time V's cells transmit her trauma to us all: June's children, and our children, and—
As in today: Call sibling in the psych ward.

WHERE: Hennepin, Nicollet, LaSalle: Minneapolis streets named for explorers. (The men always explorers.)
The Cascade Club. The Belvedere Hotel.
Minnesota Home School for Girls, Sauk Centre, Minnesota.
Probation placement: Possibly Duluth?

WHY: Because the truth was always missing. Because there is
no truth.
Because June could not bond with her children.
Because V was erased, a secret.
Because I need her to be gone.
Because I need to find her.
Because V leapt into traffic, a shock on someone's
windshield.
Because June lost V, lost her family's story.
Because we are living in V's white space
where very little can be known.

VadaVali
VanessaVelvet

VenaVera
VernaVerity

VestaVeronica
VitaVictoria

VelmaVy
VondaVilma

VickyVina
VioletVlasta

Valentine

Venus

V

How It Starts:
Minneapolis, 1935

V floats like a feather far from school. Late November loose. A pain in her back tooth that can't be fixed. Hunger acid in her belly. Her best friend Em beside her, a tether to this world.

Always V and Em end up downtown. V performing on the streets, singing for the men who still have money for young girls.

A dime a dance, Em calls. *A nickel for a song.* Em, the stubborn banker, holds the sailor cap for coins. Money they will save for a picture show and popcorn, or a quick stop at the Lolly Jar on Sixth.

V cancans and she shimmies, sings, "Ain't We Got Fun," then lands hard for a laugh. One week into fifteen, V's a red-haired Ruby Keeler, a Ziegfeld Follies hopeful sure she'll be discovered. V has what it takes to be a star.

You've got talent, one man says, his face as clean as a fresh page, his hands as smooth as snow, his thumb under her chin like a good father. (V's good father has been dead for five hard years.) *You shouldn't waste it on the street. I could put you on the stage.*

The stage? V says, her heart falling to his hands.

How much? Em asks. Em is the accountant; Em always knows exactly what V's worth.

More than this, he says, pulling a quarter from his pocket and slipping it in V's. *More than you earn now.*

The Proposition

Inside the empty Cascade Club, tiny V contemplates Mr. C's sweet proposition: Seven dollars every week, plus tips. *Can't your family use the money? Aren't times tough for a kid?*

Yes, V nods, trying to mask the thrill trapped in her throat. His offer so much better than the solo prize she won at Powderhorn last year. Nine thousand people at the park to hear her sing. V's name printed in the paper. Page 23. Her own single column clipping pressed into her scrapbook full of famous stars. Picture shows or Broadway, V dreams of either one.

Except V's not in a dream right now, she's real. Mr. C is real. This squat brick bar on Nicollet is real. Watery block windows. No bright lights marquee, but floor show posters plastered on the door. DANCING. DRINKS. HOT NIGHTS AND HAPPY GIRLS. .75 FOR FUN. No stage, he lied about the stage. The smell of last night's party wafting from the walls. Beer and whiskey. Cigarettes. Cigars. Rickety round tables with chairs stacked on the tops. A nightclub like those nightclubs where so many stars began. V knows that from the newspaper, the rags-to-riches stories of so many girls like her. Houston. Chicago. Kansas City. V's story will begin in Minneapolis.

And what about your folks? he asks, pouring V a Coca-Cola to close the deal. *I can't risk any trouble, even for a little thing like you. They going to want their pretty daughter working here?*

Sure, V lies, the heat of that last *pretty* burning her young skin. *And anyway, I mostly sleep at Em's.*

Spider bites and pinups in Em's attic, no radiator heat, but V would rather freeze than go home to that man her mother married last July. Her mother's good Norwegian-Lutheran God, gone now from their house.

You like licorice ropes and picture shows? he asks. Dark-eyed Mr. C, the handsome heartbreaker on every starlet's arm. *Silk stockings? Streetcar fare? You'll never have to walk downtown again.*

You bet, V says, but she would sing without the licorice. The street-car fare. Her body like a radio, a steady thrum of music yearning to be heard. All the dances that she's learned without a lesson longing to be seen.

V discovered at fifteen.

And so she takes the job.

Inmate's Name: V_____
Occupation: Entertainer

[Does entertainer equal
showgirl?
B-girl?
Dancer?
Singer?

Or
none of the above?

And was that V in my lost brother
with his heroin and blues?
Brother singing on the stage in Amsterdam, Munich, Paris.
Brother an entertainer at fifteen
performing on the streets of San Francisco.
Brother dead on Christmas Day.

A startling young talent
no one could account for
because no one in the family could account.]

Debut at the Cascade Club

She enters the tunnel a little fox. *Little Fox* is what he calls her, and she wears that clever nickname like a mask. Little Fox led to the light. Little Fox half-glued together with rouge, and paint, and powder. Red lips pressed to paper like a kiss.

Little Fox, he whispers, *soon you'll be my star.*

In the next room, men stripe along the bar, crowd the steamy darkness, wait for the girl to sashay into the spotlight, the girl to offer them a song. Her skin.

You'll still have your fur, he says, draping the fox stole on her shoulders, brushing his hand between her legs. *Just dance,* he says. *A dance is all they want.*

The Men of Minneapolis

Teamsters, doctors, gangsters, Nash salesmen from Harmon, reporters from the *Star,* the brakeman and the banker, the florist, the courthouse guard, the judge, the Catholics and the Jews, sullen silent Swedes, college boys with cash, Sears clerks, the candy man from Sixth, the tailor from Young-Quinlan, the doorman from the Nicollet Hotel, men who still tend horses, men who beg, men who pass a bottle at the park, the hoboes and the lawyers, the janitor from Jefferson, the Germans and the Finns, all of them pay the price to watch V sing, pay to watch her wave the sheer chiffon, flash her sequined breasts, lift her bare young legs, pay to see the glittered young girl dance. The men of Minneapolis, all hungry for V now.

Jefferson Junior High: December 1935

How little V belongs here. Orphaned mitten left in Lost and Found. Girls trade their ninth-grade gossip, while V floats off on a river, a swan that no one sees. She only comes for heat, a warm room this December. Her mother's husband drunk at home again.

Algebra and Civics, English and Life Science, steam inside V's brain, then disappear.

D and C and B and D because she's bright.

A dumb girl would be failing. A dumb girl would be caught.

Plaid skirt and schoolgirl socks, V's a master at pretending. But fifteen is a costume V can't bear.

Dull layers she will lose again tonight.

Beneath her shoe a shade of footprint.

Proof that V was here.

[Everyone who knows the truth is dead:
V
Em
the misspelled Mr. C
V's Norwegian seamstress mother
V's older sisters: Ida, Lydia, and Rose
the stepfather
the judge
the doctor who delivered June.

What I have now:
Cryptic case notes left inside V's file.
But does a file count as fact?
Or isn't every rendering a lie?]

[Let us stop to consider the stepfather—
Occupation: Disabled railroad worker. Age 53.
Or this note from the file:

"He's done all he can to help the girl."]

The Stepfather

What V hates most is his stench in their apartment. Whiskey, cigarettes, and sweat. Yellowed undershirts that reek of some dark sin. His lie that he loves V like his own daughter.

V longs to live again with only women. Poor as they were—V, her mother, and her sisters—at least V had a home. She wants the widowed years her mother raised them: boiled milk and bread for meager suppers, no drinking swearing dancing smoking, Sunday morning worship at Mindekirken Church. The black Bible always open at the bedside. An anguished Jesus in Gethsemane watching from the wall. V's bent-backed seamstress mother sewing lavish drapes and dresses for the wealthy Kenwood women. Tailoring. Repairing. V's mother up nights pinning fabric, or curved over that machine, working for her daughter's decent life.

And yet she wed this man, this disabled railroad worker, to help pay for their apartment. Pay. Which means V owes the man affection in return.

Ida, Lydia, and Rose—V's beloved sisters grown up and gone.

And V has lost her home.

And Now Among the Men

Late, V moves among the men collecting tips and tales. The longer that V listens, the more the men will pay. Addled Walt, the lonely boxer. Jean Paul, the French-Canadian, who hopped a train to nowhere and ended up in Minneapolis. V loves Jean Paul's accent. The word "Quebec." Pine and Queen. The dream of school children singing "Frère Jacques." Jean Paul who turns his pockets inside out to prove to V he's broke.

Or Ben, the widowed Baptist farmer, who carries a bottle of cheap whiskey in his coat. *The good woman wouldn't approve,* he always says, ashamed. *Do you?*

Sure thing, V says. Ben never touches V, and he tips well.

Before the Cascade Club, V saw men on the street, imagined them with strength she didn't possess, but now she sees so many as bruised children. Pouty. Full of want. Brutes, too, but V has always known that.

When one pulls V to his knee, she's quick to stand. She doesn't need to let men hold her; V can listen while they look. Hot or cold, she doesn't want to feel their calloused hands against her legs. It's only Mr. C's hands she wants now. Mr. C who always has a friendly-father wink for Little Fox.

Closer to the bar she accepts a stranger's blessing, a drunken prayer, a palm pressed to her head. V takes his nickel quickly, moves on to Soldiers' Corner in the back end of the bar. Bill who lost his right arm to the Germans. *We saved this god-damned country,* one–armed Bill insists, and men salute. *Now they left us hungry like some hoboes.*

The ruined soldiers can't tip well, but V still has a heart. On her breaks, V recites the soldiers' favorite, "Remember My Forgotten Man," and now she's mournful Joan Blondell leaning on a lamppost. Joan Blondell, a girl as poor as V who started off in vaudeville working as a circus hand and made it as a star.

V just halfway through her number, when Sven, the young flannel-shirted Swede, tells V in a slur to make a wish. *What's this?* he says, pretending to pull a penny from V's crotch.

You can keep it, V tells Sven. *Your magic and your penny. I don't need either one.*

[And why was I—
a small child without talent—
dancing at the Whirlpool,
that seedy bar off Washington
not far from where V danced?
What was I doing dancing then for tips?
At five or six or seven doing the Limbo
or the Twist to entertain old drunks.
Men with missing teeth and whiskey spit.
A small girl passed from lap to lap.
Fun June lost in conversation at the bar.
Her kids guzzling a string of kiddie cocktails.
June staying out so late we fell asleep in the back booth
with a doggie bag of ribs we ate for breakfast.
Didn't anyone know better?
Wasn't V on someone's mind?
Relatives who knew the truth of V?]

Business

V mid-song is suddenly stunned silent. Three gangsters flashing guns storm the bar for Freddy Burk.

FUCK, Freddy shouts, then scrambles from his seat, tackles toward the alley exit.

Fuck, someone else repeats. Then, *Freddy's done.*

Kid's men, a stranger whispers as he pulls V toward the floor. *Freddy must've cooked the numbers. They open fire here, we'll all be done.*

Don't shoot me, Freddy pleads, the threat of three guns pressed against his skull.

V scrambles for a spot beneath a table, watches this dark drama from the stories that she's clipped. Gangsters. Guns. Now V is in the story, another tragic showgirl. Tomorrow's headline in the paper: YOUNG STAR DEAD IN NIGHTCLUB FRAY.

Her? the kids at Jefferson will say. *That girl was a star?*

V's mother probably glad to have her showgirl daughter dead. V's sisters all ashamed. Em left without a best friend in the world.

I didn't cook nothing, Freddy weeps. *Swear to God, I didn't. You know I wouldn't do that.*

Then Mr. C, undeterred by gangsters, steps calmly from his office, lifts his gray fedora with a nod. *Gentlemen*, he says. His hand on Freddy's neck. Mr. C, always the brave father; surely he can save poor Freddy now. *Take him outside, please.*

Freddy weak-legged, wailing, dragged howling toward the exit, begging for his life. A desperate *Noooooooo* that bleeds through V.

Let's get back to business, Mr. C says. *Little Fox, these good men want a dance.*

After Hours

Emptied out and quiet, the Cascade is a land of make-believe for V and Em. (Homely Em is only welcome after close.) Mr. C in his back office balancing the books, calling out for songs from Little Fox. V proud to be his private singer, dancer. Em polishing the bar top, pretending that she works at the Cascade, too.

Pick your poison, Em tells V.

For V, a kiddie cocktail, ginger ale, a floating slip of orange, a maraschino cherry on a stick. For Em, a low-ball glass of whiskey mixed with Coca-Cola.

Just try, Em pleads, pressing the glass of fizzy booze to V's closed lips.

No, V says. Em's whiskey is the memory of V jolted out of sleep. The smell of her mother's second husband reeking at V's bedside. The man who won't have a little whore inside his house.

V turns away from Em, wipes the burn of whiskey from her lips, steals another glance at Mr. C in the side office. Mr. C too clean for beer or whiskey. Mr. C with his handsome solid face; a contour line she'd like to trace with her fox tongue. His jaw, his lips, the part between his front teeth when he laughs. His face. His hands. His hands as smooth as—

V dreams the steamy summer dream that keeps her warm this winter: V and Mr. C at Cedar Lake alone. V's costume on the shore, her hand inside of his. The cool surprise of Cedar Lake holding their great heat. V as clean as Mr. C in that dark water. A secret midnight swim the way she always did with Em, except—

Later in the sand her wet body under his. His Little Fox beneath him the way Em used to want to make believe with V.

A flock of wild birds beats in V's chest.

Wait here, V says to Em, wishing Em wouldn't be her constant shadow anymore.

At the door to his small office, V breathes in his sweet cigar and Aqua Velva, startles at the gun across his lap. *You a gangster like some say? You tied up with Kid Cann?*

You ever hear about the cat? he winks. *Curiosity? Go play with your sidekick while I work.*

You want some help counting that cash? V volunteers. V can start with counting, work forward toward the beach. *I'm good for more than songs.*

I bet you are, he says, sweeping the coins into a bag. *Ask me when you're older. My answer might be yes.*

Mr. C: Nightclub manager. Jewish. Age 35.

[Beyond those three facts of Mr. C
there is nothing I can know about this man.
The seven spellings of his name inside V's file,
all oddly missing from the Minneapolis City Directory and the
census.
Mr. C:
Northside Jew or Southside?
Romanian or German?
Immigrant or not?
Mr. C, the "handsome Jew"
V named as "special friend."
And what of all those strangers who asked June if she was Jewish?
Norwegian-Lutheran June with her lutefisk and lefse.
Or later, asked us if we were.
Us, a pack of Irish-Catholic kids?]

Generosity: January 1936

1.

V with the kindness of fifteen, concocts a pot of onion soup for Mr. C,
adds a pinch of pepper while Em stirs. V and Em are young chefs skipping school. (Em's waitress mother gone all day at work.)

When the time comes to deliver, V insists she'll take the soup to Mr.
C alone. Two girls will be too much for a man sick with pneumonia. Em
fights, but V holds firm. She packs the steaming pot into a box, steals
a bowl and spoon from Em, leaves Em at the sink with a stack of dirty
dishes to be washed.

At the paper stand on Lyndale, V buys a *Tribune* for Mr. C.

In her father's final days, he liked V to sit beside his bed to read the
Book of Psalms.

2.

V with the kindness of fifteen, standing in the hallway of the Belvedere
Hotel. Her red hair in snowy ringlets, a goofy young girl grin.

Soup, she says, *I heard that you were sick.*

Mr. C in those strange cotton-pant pajamas, a matching shirt. Nearly
naked without his strict black suit and tie.

Does your teacher know you're here? He coughs.

Mr. C, exactly like her mother, always telling V to stay in school.

I brought you the Tribune, she says nodding toward the paper, looking past his striped pajamas to his private hotel life lit by one dim bulb. *I could read you the paper while you rest. Serve you soup in bed.*

You should go, he says, glancing down the vacant hallway, first right, then left, before he lets V step inside.

3.

Exactly as she'd dreamed when she left Em angry in that kitchen. Exactly as she'd dreamed walking three long miles to the Belvedere Hotel.

4.

[The kindness of fifteen. The hangman thirty-five.]

5.

6.

[I know what you think.]

7.

Afterward V closes like a zipper, her dream complete; Mr. C a snake she captured in the woods. The onion soup cold now on the table. V's wrinkled blouse lost in his white sheets. The crumpled *Tribune* thrown open on the floor.

V weaves her slender fingers between his, rests her cheek against his fevered chest, draws a threaded needle between her heart and his.

You're mine, she sighs, flexing up on one bare elbow to study his dark face.

To stare long into love.

Fifteen.

Sweetheart, Mr. C says with a wheeze. *You're young enough to be my kid.*

I know, V says, wishing that she was.

[TRUE OR FALSE]

1. T F The author is deliberately deceptive.
2. T F The author does not know the truth and so she lies.
3. T F The author trusts fiction over fact.
4. T F The author wants the truth, but knows she'll never have it.
5. T F There is a truth the author knows, but she can't tell.
6. T F The author was taught early not to tell.

Generosity Revised

[Or this version based on facts—?

                                        After fact, everything is fiction.]

Spring mist, a January trick, and V befuddled by a Life Science test on cells, decides to skip another day of school, walk the city alleys toward LaSalle. A secret maze of strangers' garbage that leads to Mr. C.

Mr. C asleep at the Belvedere Hotel.

[For this version, let's agree this visit's not V's first. She knows the corner building on LaSalle, the heavy door, the beveled window, the mildew smell of the front lobby, the flirty bow-tied boy at the front desk. V will never date a bow-tied boy again.]

Inside, she takes the shadowed hallway to the right. Morning *Tribunes* dropped outside closed doors. Smell of shaving soap and showers, and the murmur of low radios floating from the rooms. A place she'd like to live if he'd just ask.

At 106, V's knock is soft and loose and full of hope. Last time she skipped school, he looped his arm around her waist, swept her in before another hotel tenant called the cops.

Mr. C is thirty-five and Jewish in a town against the Jews. (GENTILES PREFERRED; V has read the ads.) V's fifteen, a girl in junior high. The cops get wind of this, he'll land in jail. Men he knows have served time for carnal knowledge.

Carnal knowledge: two words that make V dangerous and dark. Caramel knowledge. A sweet subject to be studied, and he does.

No school? He blinks, surprised.

Life Science, she says, shrugging. *I don't understand a cell.*

No? He smiles. *I can help with that.*

[And why dream them into being?
This man?
That girl?
My mother's lost beginning?
Hotel or not? Mr. C or someone else?

That cell:
To understand that cell.]

"The fateful meeting of the sperm and the ovum takes place usually in the upper end of one of the fallopian tubes. It is a wonderful occasion."

—*William S. Sadler and Lena K. Sadler,*
The Mother and Her Child, *1916*

Pinned

The first gift that he gives her is a dress clip. Costume jewelry fancy. Teardrop amethyst. Silver filigree. The two of them snowed-in inside the Cascade Club alone. The winter city stalled and buried under white.

For me? V says, surprised. After shows, men shower V with gifts— red carnations, dolls, and candy—but V will never be their girl. *I don't need a gift.*

I know, he winks. His beautiful black eyes exactly like the raven in that poem V's eighth-grade teacher made her memorize last year.

Evermore, she says, but he just laughs. *Like Edgar Allan Poe.*

I know that, too, he says. *I went to school once. And it was nevermore in my book.*

But evermore for us, V says.

Sure, he says. *Why not?* He clips the pin on her lapel like a medal V has earned.

For what? V asks. *It's not my birthday 'til November.* She's told him that before, but maybe he forgot.

Sweet sixteen. You'll have a hundred high school boys with trinkets for you then.

V knows that isn't true, but it's a lie she likes to hear and so she leaves it.

When you wear it think of me. His hand over her breast, his thumb across her nipple, his lips moving on V's neck the way she loves.

Who else, but you? V answers, her hungry tongue darting out toward his, her fingers on his face, the jeweled clip a gift she'll love for evermore.

Outside the empty bar the winter night is silent. Cars abandoned under drifts. A quilt of blizzard snow over the street, the avenue deserted. Em at home in bed where she belongs. (V doesn't want Em stopping after hours anymore. Em can see her in the morning; morning is enough.)

You think we'll have to sleep here? V asks, nudging his suspender off his shoulder.

Sleep? He smiles. *I don't think that's in the cards.*

The Evidence of Love

Young V collects the evidence of love: His hotel window slammed against the winter draft, the way he curves his hands around her hips. How he asks her if it hurts, and hopes for no. The tender way he rests her back first on his bed, his left hand behind her head and whispers, *Baby*. How he bit the middle button from her blouse, a good luck charm V later found in his front pocket. How his dark eyes follow V as she works the Cascade Club. V the tiny vixen that belongs to Mr. C. Belongs. And doesn't that mean love?

[Or do I collect the evidence of love?
Mr. C among V's first explorers.

Me, seventy-five years later
looking for the subtext as I've trained myself to do.

The writer whose job it is to excavate.

The writer always looking
for that man inside her mirror.

That man of minor honor.

I invent his minor honor.
I invent it all.]

You Stay Safe?

In the early winter darkness, V shivers between houses, waits until her mother's husband limps down Emerson toward Topps. That checkered cap, that leg. Always on his way to get a drink. Inside the basement hallway, his stench of menthol salve.

For you, V says, forcing a twenty-dollar bill into her mother's wrinkled hand. The youngest daughter of the family, but V is finally old enough to help. *I'm earning money now. Enough that we could move. Move from him.*

Move? her mother says. *I can't just leave Ray, V.*

Still, her mother hides the twenty-dollar bill safe inside her ragged bra without asking how V earns it, kisses V's cheek as a thank you, tucks a strand of curls behind V's ear. *You stay safe?* She isn't asking for an answer. *You're up with Em now in her attic? You be good with Em.* V's mother doesn't want to hear the truth about her girl. *You could come home to your family. A girl belongs at home.*

Not now, V says. *You know I hate it here.*

I wish—her mother weeps. V lets her mother cry—a sign her mother might be sorry. Remorse for that wrong marriage is all V really wants. Remorse and curiosity. Just once, V wants to hear her mother ask: *What did my second husband do to you, sweet daughter?*

But V's mother never asks. Not tonight. [Not later when V leaps.] Her mother leaves that truth unspoken as a dare. Daring V to tell her. Daring V to say: *I'm bad fruit your second husband handled.*

You and Em must go to school, her mother says, struggling the cast iron soup pot from the stove into the sink. *Good girls go to school. I don't want a letter from the principal again.*

I go to school, V sighs, sure that she's been asked again to keep the second husband's secret.

His secret, and whatever secret brought those twenty dollars to her door.

Truancy

V arrives at school, but cannot stay. Second period, while Em is gone to Lower English, V slips down the vacant north-end stairwell, and bolts for Mr. C at the Belvedere Hotel.

Mr. C with the taste of buttered toast still on his tongue, his olive skin a winter cure for V. A morning goblet of warm milk beside the bed for V's good health.

Mr. C who arranges naked V on his settee and calls her Venus. Mr. C who says she should be art.

Nothing but that man can hold her now. Not loyal Em with her young clowning, not junior high with its Civil War and Shakespeare, not her old-world mother who fears V's truancy's a crime. *Good girls go to school. You be a good girl.*

Only Mr. C and their perfect, private mornings unfolding at the Belvedere Hotel.

The First Day V Suspects

The third of March and snow ponds on the sidewalk. A man smoking on his balcony leans low and whistles twice. *Ain't you the Cascade Fox?* he calls to V, but V just walks. She needs a bigger city like New York. A Broadway club called Foxy's owned by Mr. C. V a story in the scrapbook of another dreaming girl. "Dashing Mr. C and His Young Beauty Take the Town."

Hey, little girl, the stranger calls again. *I know I seen you dance.*

Suddenly, a lurch inside her stomach, not butterflies, but dropping, like the time she tumbled from the tree at Bryant Square.

V hurries onto the streetcar, the seats all full, the weary passengers worn thin from work. The boy ahead of V digs into his pockets. No money and no token, so V quickly pays his fare. *I'll take care of it,* V says gently, the way a mother might.

No, V is not a mother.

Still, she senses a small nub inside her soul, an uninvited second spirit, a light illuminating all that is behind her and ahead. Light invisible. Unwanted.

V swallows down her spit, ignores the nagging knowledge of that nub. A stray cat scratch at her door. V could kill the cat, flounce down the streetcar stairs into the dusk, her handbag swinging at her hip, parade into the Cascade as the wild Little Fox. A reckless showgirl happily half-dressed, her winter coat at home, brand-new Oxfords stained with melted snow. The girl men pay to see. Men don't pay to see a mother dance.

Before the streetcar reaches Franklin, V decides to be that girl again.

[V invented out of what?
Changed addresses. Four apartments
in five years listed in the file.
Possibly evictions?

Uptown, Loring, Phillips.
Minneapolis neighborhoods
where V and I both lived.
My own apartments so like V's.
The first basement apartment after June's divorce.
Musty childhood home.
Strangers' shoes glimpsed through narrow windows.

I create from clippings. Scrapbook work.
Evidence uncovered:
The city solo contest in 1933.
V performing for nine thousand and taking home the prize.

V, collaged from my own life at fifteen.
Smoking on the lawn at Holy Angels.
Shut inside a closet when I didn't behave in class.
Greyhound bus to California.
Skipping school for beers at Westrum's bar.

V inspired by nightclub ads and 1930s movies.
Matchbook covers. A faded postcard of Mr. C's hotel.

Now an apartment on LaSalle where I loiter in the lobby
willing V to walk out of his room.

V mirroring my mother,
pregnant at fifteen because
the daughter must resemble—

Or invented from my classmate Patty Darling,
who disappeared sophomore year with her night boss from
McDonald's.
The blank space that straight-A Patty left behind.

V collaged from pieces that I paste into a girl.]

First Offense

[Here let us reconstruct the crime.]

1.

V and Em, young and loose on another day of hooky, stroll the March-mud streets of Minneapolis, soak up the city symphony of cars, the welcome honks from strangers meant for V, the screech of streetcars coming to a stop. Em in ragged boy-pants she found at Bethel Charity. V with freckled bare legs, winter white. Their bulky boots abandoned. A stripe of flowered summer skirt beneath V's coat. Spring fever and it isn't even spring.

Em says a day like this demands a lark like Lu's apartment. Lu in South Dakota with her folks. A prank that Lu will love, Em's sure of that.

Em knows the secret way in through the alley. Nights while V's performing at the Cascade, Lu's the friend Em likes to run with now. A better pal than V.

But didn't V give up the Belvedere to spend the day with Em?

Em finds the hidden milk crate stashed behind the trash, climbs the crate, gives the unlocked window one strong nudge. *You first,* she says to V, cupping her hands into a stirrup to give V one big boost. V tumbling head-first onto Lu's apartment floor. Behind V, hearty Em landing with a thud. The two of them so thrilled with this adventure, Em pees her baggy pants. So drunk with wild laughter they don't wonder at the neighbor who hears them through the wall.

While Em strips out of her wet pants and into Lu's pajamas, V ransacks the tidy kitchen for a stale, half-burnt biscuit and a jar of cherry jam. A dish of thick canned peaches from the cupboard in the hall.

Won't Lu love this lark? Em says, happier than V has seen her since the Cascade visits stopped. Em lifts Lu's satin quilt to make room for waitress V. *Won't she be surprised that we were here?*

You know it, V says, handing Em their scavenged picnic, then climbing in beside her, her cheek against Em's arm just like old times.

Lu can't be a better pal than me, V says. Lu Nyquist with her boring Baptist parents, the fancy prism lamps beside her bed, a silver-plated brush V plans to steal. V shoves a piece of sticky biscuit into Em's always open mouth. *Lu wouldn't do a lark like this with you.*

2.

Later, V trembles in a cop car while Em jokes that they're two jailbirds, begs the cop for handcuffs because it's always been her dream. She wants to see the Big House for herself. Get a file in a cake. Go on the lam. Em telling the cop that Lu's nosy neighbor ought to learn to mind his own biz. They had Lu's permission to play hooky at her house.

You're a regular Jack Benny, the cop says to shut up Em. He's had it with her chatter: her fake addresses, fake names. Thirty-Fifth and Portland. Eighteenth Avenue. Twenty-Eighth and Park. She's Mary Christmas. V's Eileen Sideways. Hahaha. A wild goose chase to locate parents, but he's done with fun and games. He can't blow his whole day driving two dumb broads through town. Better looking than the bums, but still he drops them at the station and leaves them with, *Good luck.*

Fingerprints and phone calls. Mr. C won't answer; Em's mother can't be found. Hours later, it's V's mother, her own stomach sick with shame, who begs the cop to release V to her home. V's mother who swears that V's a good girl. All her girls are good. V's mother with the husband right beside her, already whiskey-soaked from Topps, insisting they should send V to detention, saying he won't have a whore inside his house.

3.

On the street outside the station, he slaps V across the face. *Whore,* he says again, and he should know. *You want the belt, too, V? You want it now?*

Be good now, V, her mother frets, stepping in between her daughter and that man. *You don't want to be a bad girl.*

I do, V says. *Why not?*

4.

And who will dance for Mr. C tonight?

". . . The term delinquent child shall mean a child who violates any law of this state

or any city or village ordinance;

or who is habitually truant or incorrigible;

or who knowingly associates with vicious or immoral persons;

or who without just cause and without the consent of his parents, guardian, or other custodian absents himself from his home or place of abode,

or who knowingly visits any place which exists,

or where his presence is permitted,

in violation of law;

or who habitually uses obscene, profane, or indecent language;

or who is guilty of lewd or immoral conduct involving another person."

—*William H. Mason, "Chapter 73A; Dependent, Neglected and Delinquent Children,"* Mason's Minnesota Statutes, *1927*

Reformed

1.

V, trying to climb back from delinquent, attends school like a good girl, completes her daily homework, goes to bed in that apartment with her mother's sewing scissors in her hand. He touches her again she'll take his heart.

Sunday mornings, feigning purity, she sings beside her mother at Mindekirken Church. In that stony, steepled house of stiff wood pews and stained-glass windows, V stumbles through the hymns in strange Norwegian. Prays the little she remembers: *La ditt navn holdes heelig. La ditt rike komme.*

Kill this cell, she adds silently, in case God really hears.

Then, *Please God, let Mr. C be there Monday,* because sometimes now he is. Monday, Tuesday, Wednesday; V is never sure. But there is Mr. C as a surprise: Waiting in his black Ford after school, parked on Emerson or Fremont, or across the street from Jefferson to be sure V's staying true. He doesn't want some ninth-grade punk walking his girl home. Mr. C forcing V to take his money because he knows she needs it now. Reminding V to keep his secrets. Their secrets. Each time warning V to steer clear of the law.

When things quiet with the cops, he'll be waiting at the Belvedere for V. A month or two without more trouble, and V will star again as Little Fox.

2.

Saturdays, V spends his money on a matinee and more. First, Chesterfields for Em. For V, a cape trimmed with silver fox fur. Fake, but Em swears V wears it well. Chocolate balls and taffy, peppermints and popcorn, treats that they can feast on through the show. V and Em just like the old days, curled up in the velvety day-darkness of the Uptown, Em practicing her smoke rings while V dreams of her future as a dancer in New York. The blinding costume of gold coins she'll get to wear. V another girl about to make it big.

Don't worry, V, Em whispers in the darkness. *You can marry Mr. C and be a mother.*

Clever Em who somehow sees the truth that V can't say. Sees that secret cell.

No, V says. *That isn't what I want.*

3.

Afterwards V vomits in the street. Chocolate balls and popcorn bits splattered on V's boots.

[And what does V want at fifteen if not motherhood and marriage?
To have her worthy talent acknowledged by the world?
To use the gifts that she was given?

My own dream at fifteen, not to sing, but to write.

Did V dream beyond the Cascade
yet settle for a brothel
like so many shining talents of her time?

Because the artist must begin her work where she can.

V burning with the stage-dream my brother chased to Europe.
Or later still the song and dance obsession consuming my
young son.
Tap-shoe boy at three,
fixated on Tchaikovsky.
At ten, phoning for auditions
he'd found in the *Star Tribune*.

Boy dreaming the same V dream.
Boy who didn't begin as Little Fox.]

The Last Good Day

Forever they will have this last good day.

The smell of melted snow through his propped window, a closed rose between V's breasts, the sweet strain of a Victrola through the vent.

Mr. C telling V her beauty should be bronzed, her flock of perfect freckles, her flawless child face.

V flutters her sure fingers through his forest of dark chest hair, presses her hot palm against his heart to feel it beat.

Always that strong heart.

I want you to just love me, V says. *For evermore.*

Sure thing, he says. *But forever is a long time when you're young.*

Luck

Leaving the Belvedere at lunch time, V runs out of luck. The crabby cop that caught V and Em in Lu's apartment is standing on LaSalle. *Well, Eileen Sideways,* he says with a mean smirk. *Half-past noon on Wednesday? Shouldn't you be in school?*

Across the street, the man huddled in the blanket lifts his head to listen. He's been watching V all winter; he knows where V has been.

You know someone in that place? the cop asks V. *Maybe that fella from the Cascade? The one with all the liquor violations? You come to see him here?*

No, V lies. How does this cop know Mr. C? The Cascade Club? *I stepped in to use the toilet.*

Long time to pee. He studies V's new cape, the fake fox fur, the silk stockings that she wore for Mr. C, the fancy high-heeled Oxfords her school wouldn't allow. *I saw you slip in there this morning.*

This morning? V repeats like he's confused. She knows better than to glance over her shoulder, to look up toward Mr. C spying through the crack of his closed curtain. He always watches for V's wave when she crosses on LaSalle.

A lady thing. V blushes, embarrassed. *I didn't feel up to school, so I stopped here. My girlfriend has a place.*

I bet she does. Good old Mary Christmas? And what room number would that be?

Six twenty-three, V lies again, hoping if he knocks that guest is gone.

Sure, he says. *Just like you lived on Elliot. And Oakland. And every other street you had me chasing to that day.* He squints his eyes at V, bends low to her face, lifts her nervous chin to sniff her breath for booze. *What are you, thirteen? Fourteen?* He clicks his tongue, tugs the brim of his flat cap. *You know I got a girl your age.*

You do? V says, relieved he has a daughter. A father might be kinder. Her father would be kind. *She go to Jefferson like me? Ninth grade? Home-room Mrs. Paisley?*

You're a damn far way from homeroom, he says, taking a long, slow glance at the seven floors of curtained windows on LaSalle. *Six twenty-three?* he says, suspicious. *Girls get started on the wrong foot, who knows where they end up.*

Life Science

A full investigation into charges will be made: immorality, truancy, whatever shady business V had in that hotel—but first while V's in custody, the county doctor must determine if the rabbit lives or dies.

It's routine, the awkward county doctor says. He's college-young, baby-faced, in-training, eager to return to his family farm in Windom. *Good clean living in the country. You ought to try it out.* He tells all this to V with his fat cheeks burning red.

When was your last? he asks. *You know, any blood down there that you remember?*

V's desperate for a memory of blood, the sludge-soaked cloth between her legs, but all the days and nights since Mr. C have been a blur.

Last month? V lies. *I'm still too young to be regular. I only got my visitor last year.* Too young. The same excuse she gives Mr. C when he asks her why she doesn't bleed like other girls.

A river of fresh sweat runs down her ribs onto the table. No blood-smeared sheets with Mr. C, that much V knows. He doesn't want her girl-stains on his mattress, her blood to touch his skin. Once, in the storeroom of the Cascade, he felt the shame between her legs, then washed his hands with whiskey while V watched.

Not last month, the county doctor says, laying his hand over V's abdomen. *I can feel a hill already.*

That's food, V says. *I've had the money to eat more.* Same thing she says to Mr. C when he asks about the weight.

The doctor glances down V's gown to see her swollen breasts. *And those,* he says. *Can't you see they're awfully big for a small girl? What are you, ninety pounds? The Women's Bureau will want names—*

But I'm not, V pleads, before he has a chance to finish. College boys have liked her at the Cascade, the rich ones have tipped well. *I could get my monthly any minute. And isn't there a way? You know? Something with a wire? A tea girls drink?*

Last year homely Donna Rice got sentenced to the state school for eight years for being pregnant. Her empty choir chair was a sin for all to see. If there really is a baby, V needs it to be gone.

A wire? he says, worried. *Don't ever try that trick.*

V shivers as he writes that in her record. *Not that, please,* V begs. *I honestly didn't mean it. You can cross that last part out.*

I wish I could, he says, concerned. *But the Women's Bureau needs to know the trouble with you girls.*

Not with me, V says. *I don't have any trouble.* Whatever trouble he discovers can quickly disappear. V heard that a waitress at the Cascade "was," then wasn't. Mr. C can end it; he'll know someone who will.

What V Knows from
Her Clippings

Any star can fall.

Don't lose your heart or your head.

A girl needs courage.

Put on a costume. Get to work.

A determined girl moves on from heartbreaks.

Remember men act foolishly. Don't be a foolish girl.

Keep your sights set on the stage.

The world rewards a smile.

Applause can't last.

Don't dally at a table full of drunks.

Lots of girls have looks and talent.

A figure only goes so far, but a showgirl won't go far without her figure.

Girls are always waiting in the wings.

When a star runs into trouble, she should take it like a champ.

[INCIDENTAL EVIDENCE]

Girls and women who become mothers out of wedlock may be divided into the following types:

(a) The mentally subnormal girl who lacks controlling inhibitory instincts and is an easy victim because of helplessness;

(b) the young, susceptible girl, unprotected from dangers, who gets into trouble because of lack of understanding, or through force;

(c) the more mature young woman of good character who is led by false promises or who weakly or rashly follows an instinct that under other conditions would have been normal and social;

(d) the really delinquent girl or woman, who knowingly chooses antisocial conduct, her illegitimate maternity being only an incidental evidence of repeated immorality.

> —*Emma O. Lundberg,* Children of Illegitimate Birth and Measures for Their Protection, *Bureau Publication No. 166, U.S. Department of Labor, Children's Bureau, 1926*

Consolation Mr. C

Of course, Mr. C can't find a doctor or propose. Not with V fifteen, the court involved, the cops, a baby on the way she can't abort. A short stint at the state school and the worst of this will pass.

Behind him the night laughter of drunk men escapes the Cascade Club. At V's wet feet, the alley puddles blue with melted snow. Oil rainbows and bar garbage is how V will think of spring.

Spring, a season V will finish someplace else.

Is she his Freddy Burk now? She can almost feel the press of gun against her skull. She's a girl without a suitcase, a girl who needs to dig her way to Timbuktu or China.

But I don't want to go, V says, swallowing her sob.

You're a few years short of marriage, kid.

This isn't about marriage. It's V caged until she's twenty-one. V caged while Mr. C—

The county could commit me for six years.

Mr. C's a man of means. He owns a Ford, a wallet thick with bills. He knows businessmen and bootleggers from California to New York, men building a bright city called Las Vegas. He could run away with V before tomorrow's hearing. V's sister Rose lives in Milwaukee; they can hide with Rose.

Six years, V repeats. Six years ago, she played with Ziegfeld paper dolls and patterns. She started that stupid scrapbook about showgirls, their tragedies and triumphs, while dreaming of her own. Six years from now—

Who will that V be?

Don't worry, Mr. C soothes, taking the starched kerchief from his pocket to dab at V's wet cheeks like she's a child. She is a child. *You go off and lay that robin's egg. Get done with that, and then you can come home.*

In this hushed library of history, pale wooden tables and chairs, a cardboard box of fragile documents delivered by the clerk, I sit beside my gray-haired mother poring over papers for the story of her birth. A state-held mother-daughter puzzle made from yellowed scraps.

Baby _ _ _ _ _ _ _ _ **1936.** June's adoption record sealed by law for one hundred silent years, but steely June has pried it open with a letter to the court. A plea to know her truth before a century has passed. The court can do the math; in 2036 June will be dead.

June stares down at her slim archive, studies buried facts and data trying to find the story. Familiar names and addresses. Faint type-written notes we struggle to decipher. Words gone with time and now are lost.

She was dancing at fifteen? June says with concern. *Singing? At the Cascade Club on Nicollet? And he was thirty-five?* June, the dispassionate accountant, distressed by addition and subtraction, by the numbers in her file that lead to a father.

And this! June says, her shocked whisper pulling me from my own pages, causing quiet patrons to turn toward June's alarm. June's palm pressed to her chest as if an accident has occurred. *Until twenty-one,* she says with disbelief. *V was sentenced until twenty-one, for what?*

June passes me the judgment, points to that terrible wording that commits her ninth-grade mother as an inmate for six years. *For me,* June says, answering her own question with an unfamiliar mix of guilt and sadness. *Six years for being pregnant? Can you imagine at fifteen?*

No, I lie, because I'm already imagining a fifteen-year-old dancer, imagining the Sauk Centre institution where baby June was born.

[HERE THE WRITER TURNS TO RESEARCH]

- Mason's Minnesota Statues 1927. Supplement 1936.
- Laws of other states.
- Books on girls. Girls as entertainers. Delinquents. Reformatories. Unwed mothers 1935. The history of unwed mothers.
- Juvenile crime in Minnesota.
- Antisemitism in Minneapolis 1930s. (Why the many mentions of "Jews" inside V's file?)
- Minneapolis liquor violations: Cascade Club.
- Organized crime in Minneapolis.
- Carnal knowledge.
- Adjudication of paternity.
- Bastards.
- History of prisons Minnesota. History of prisons.
- History of girls.
- History as context, not conclusion, because so little of this history is true.

Finding of Facts

First, the air lost from V's lungs. A quiver in her heart that can't be heard. The county courtroom closing on all sides.

Then the fat judge makes a joke about fast girls, and someone laughs. Her stepfather. Yes, the disabled railroad worker is laughing with the judge. And he's done all he can to help the girl.

Her mother's narrow face folds to a frown. The distance between her heart and V's is a sea that V can't cross.

The girl's a deviant and truant, her mother's husband says. Every fact the county found against V is in the record now. The Cascade Club. The dancing. This pregnancy. The day she stayed too long inside the Belvedere Hotel. *A showgirl at that club run by the Jews. She's been immoral with those men and now she's pregnant. My good wife is too lenient. She can't control the child.*

What's the matter with you girls? The judge shakes his head disgusted. V's sorry for so much, but she can't say it. *Half-dressed and entertaining drunks just to earn a dime. Pregnant with a child this country can't afford.*

V can't afford it either.

Gonorrhea. Syphilis. Who knows what diseases— The stepfather again. *She's worse than weekend sailors—*

I don't have— V interrupts, because she doesn't.

You don't have common decency, the judge says before V can correct him. *But you'll learn it at the state school. They'll see to it you do. Twenty-one,* he orders, scrawling his name across a paper V will never see. *I hope that baby finds a family. I hope to God it's not another girl.*

Guardianship

Because no crime has been committed, because a house has not been robbed, because nothing has been vandalized or stolen, and no one has been harmed, except for V, there is no crime for which she has been charged.

Instead the state commits V as IMMORAL: an offense against society. An offense reserved for girls. (Or Incorrigible/Immoral, depending on the class.) Delinquent boys are arsons, fighters, thieves.

The state so much better suited than V's working, widowed mother (an eighth-grade education, foreign born, a seamstress) to reform a wayward girl.

[The crime is Mr. C's,
but do you think he served six years?]

[THE WRITER TRIES TO MAKE SENSE OF THE LAW]

The law authorizes the school to receive girls between the ages of eight and eighteen
    [eight and eighteen]
    upon commitment by a juvenile court
    commitment [consignment to a penal or mental institution]
    after a finding of delinquency
    delinquency [behavior especially by the young, that is antisocial]
    The commitment proceedings are in the nature of guardianship hearings
    guardian [a person who guards, protects, or takes care of another]
    and do not constitute a criminal record
    criminal [involving illegal activities]
    The guardianship may be extended until a child is twenty-one years of age
    [twenty-one years of age]

        —Handbook of American Institutions for Delinquent Juveniles,
                Vol. 1: West North Central States, 1938

"The commitment proceedings are in the nature of guardianship hearings and do not constitute a criminal record."

—Handbook of American Institutions for Delinquent Juveniles,
Vol. 1: West North Central States, 1938

The Last Gift That
He Gives Her

A teardrop necklace. Costume jewelry cheap. Rhinestone blue and common; V has seen the same on other girls.

She rolls it between her thumb and fingers like a thing that she doesn't want.

I wish I could do more, he says. *I do.* A lie so weak, V vows in that moment to forget it's what he said. Those words, and his impatient, perfect knuckles drumming on the desk. Mr. C so obviously eager for the last of V to end. *I'll come to visit when I can,* he says rising from his desk chair. His eyes already leaving V and looking toward the door. *You keep our secret, Little Fox, we'll be together.*

How? V asks. She tries to slit her thumb on the sharp edge of the rhinestone. No blood, the stone still teardrop blue. He can give it to another girl. He will.

You wait and see, he says, rushing V out toward the alley, giving her a bird kiss before he opens the back door. *I might be a man of minor honor, but sometimes minor honor is enough.*

Were

Fallen woman. Fallen girl. Fallen from the grace of God. Parading like a peacock. Bringing home sin money from those men.

This is what V's mother says, as she snips a keepsake souvenir of V's red curls, returns the scissors to the basket for tomorrow's seamstress work.

I remember who you were. You were the apple of my eye. Your good sisters never would have done so wrong.

Now V is wrong and were. Someone past. Someone loved and lost. Her last supper of chipped beef simmers on the stove. Her oldest sister Lydia on the way to say good-bye. Rose married in Milwaukee. Ida in Cheyenne with a baby of her own.

Tonight, the railroad worker's gone to Topps, and V is glad.

Tonight, he'll try to visit V in bed and call her *whore.*

Once you were a good girl, V's mother says, confused. *Reading on that rag rug. Always* Little Women.

For so long V played the role of pampered Amy. But weren't they all the March girls, industrious and brave, learning to make do without a father?

What happened to that girl? her mother asks, sealing V's curl into an envelope she'll find in thirty years.

Where did that girl go?

[Where did that girl go?
Those girls?
V not only V now.
V, yes, but V also a statistic.
V about to be a girl among the thousands who were held.
June about to be a baby among babies
whose birth stories can't be known.
Stories sealed into silence.
But wasn't that the point?]

[EVIDENCE OF V: 1970, DOWNTOWN MINNEAPOLIS

On a sick day home from school, accountant June is home, too—an anomaly, June never misses work. June takes me on an errand, for what she will not say. There is no reason that June should want me with her. June prefers to leave her children, sick or not. And yet, this day, June oddly needs me near. Needs me with her at the counter once her number has been called. It's her birth certificate she's after; I'm twelve, so that much I understand. The wait is slow. Already, the customers behind us have been helped. I'm fever-sweating in my turtleneck and Levi's, the fake-rabbit-fur cropped jacket June gave to me on Christmas. (My *sister* gave to me on Christmas; my older sister shops for June.)

When the clerk finally returns, the birth certificate she offers June is wrong. *This isn't it,* June says. June's a force; if she wants a different piece of paper the clerk should find one fast. I want to warn the nervous clerk, but I stand quiet. *This can't be mine,* June says. *I'm thirty-three; I should know where I was born. I wasn't born in Sauk Centre.* The nervous clerk is sorry, very sorry. *There must be some mistake,* June says, *go back and look again.*

My fever, I remind June, tugging on the sleeve of her old coat. Everyone is watching; but watching won't stop June. June doesn't give a shit what people think, and we shouldn't either.

Look, June insists. *Go back and look again.*

Madame, you should leave. Now it's a man who tries to quiet June. Man-ager. *This is all that we can give you. Do you want your birth certificate or not?*

Go to hell, June says, *I don't need a man to tell me*—but then she grabs the paper, storms out of that office leaving me to trail. (All my life I trail June.)

This much I know for certain: That birth certificate, it isn't what June wants. That's what I'll remember. That, and June folding that horrible paper into thirds like a letter she won't read. June stone silent until the elevator empties, but then that whispered warning: *Don't you ever tell a living soul what we did today. Not a living soul.*

I won't, I promise June, proud to share her secret.

Unsure for years of what our secret is.]

II.

AND HER THERE
SAFELY KEEP

In the name of the STATE OF MINNESOTA, you, the said SHERIFF are hereby commanded and required forthwith to convey the said _____ into the custody of the Superintendent of the Home School in Sauk Centre, Stearns County, Minnesota; and you, the said SUPERINTENDENT are hereby commanded to receive the said _____ into your custody, and her there safely keep until she shall become 21 years of age.

—Found legal document

[ERASURE: THE SUPERINTENDENT SPEAKS]

"now that I may keep to my subject   I may show you in a more intensive way the purpose of our institution   our Minnesota Home School
state institution for delinquent girls   on petition or complaints of par-
ent, guardian, or officer of the law, any girl   if found guilty of incorrigibility, immorality, vagrancy   nor is an actual offense always a necessity
girls have been sent to us   "in danger of becoming delinquent, incorrigible, immoral"   while by law all commitments must be "until the
age of twenty-one"   following an intensive training in the institution
the girl   is paroled by the board   to a home or occupation of the
state's finding   in our school at Sauk Centre 310 girls with 270 under
our care in the community   the motive of the institution   a social
readjustment of the girl   who through disadvantage has become a
social offender or social misfit   its purpose the making of decent wives
and mothers and home-makers   built on the cottage plan   each such
cottage represents an independent family unit or group   family room,
dining room, kitchen, and individual sleeping rooms   scattered over
large acreage of open space and woodland   administration building,
hospital, chapel, and farm buildings   mention should be made here
of our colony for the young unmarried mother   a mile and a half from
the institution proper   added to this group, supplementing and
humanizing   another group of our girls, who because of mental de-
fect, should not be returned to the community   the latter we term the
non-social group   the advantages of the cottage system   segregation

into small groups   according to former experiences and offense so complete is our segregation   many a girl on the completion of her training goes out   ignorant of the names of the mass of girls outside her cottage group   society's greatest need today is the home   to grow in the girl this home sense: a consciousness of the possibilities of a home, a desire for it   how to fulfill it   the home as a factor in the building of women   the girl's first loaf of bread is to her a greater pride than is many a college diploma   farm work and gardens, planting of shrubbery and trees, mowing of lawns   as a means of humanizing the girl   I refer to the actual production which the farm labor of our girls today represents   this last year over 900 acres were cared for; over 500 acres of this under field and garden cultivation   largely the work of the girls   thousands of quarts of vegetables have been canned   the educational department lends itself almost entirely to the one purpose of the institution, training for home life   education through books is a slow process nor have most of our girls a basis for such   to what degree is our work proving good?   all success is relative, but would you count a mean accomplishment the rehabilitation of a home by a girl of fifteen; the carrying back   family standards and domestic values no girl leaves   without a higher ideal   that in the inevitable, natural force of things must somewhere, somehow, some time find expression. A denial of this would be a denial of the eternal."

—*Fannie French Morse, First Superintendent, Minnesota Home School for Girls at Sauk Centre. Excerpted from* Proceedings of the First State Conference of Child Welfare Boards with The Board of Control, State Capitol, May 9 and 10, 1919, *St. Paul, Minnesota, 1919*

Morse Hall, Minnesota Home School for Girls at Sauk Centre, ca. 1939

And Her There Safely Keep

1.

Not bad for the pen, the sheriff jokes.

Through the window of the backseat, V takes in the Minnesota Home School for Girls at Sauk Centre. A school that's not a school; a home that's not her home. Farmland and flat sky as far as V can see. The same stink of so much country she's had to breathe these depressing hours in the car. Cows or pigs or corn, she doesn't recognize the stench. She's never spent a day out on a farm, and now she will be held here in these fields trapped in silence.

Shady clusters of dark trees. An immaculate green lawn. Leafy lilac shrubs. A scattering of clapboard houses standing lonely on the land. No house next to another. No one near to hear V scream. No alleys. No streetcar V can hop to Minneapolis when she's ready to be done. No Olson's Grocer on the corner. No Sears. No shops of any kind. No kids chasing down the street. No streets. No Cascade Club. No Mr. C. No Em. No mother. No older, doting sisters to spring V from this mess. A world so far from love and freedom V could crack.

No one who V loves will find her here.

Please don't leave me here, V begs, choking back a sob. Her hand touching his right shoulder in case a girl's small hand will help. *I can't stay at this school, I just can't.*

You'll straighten out, the sheriff says, slowing to a stop. *It's a good place for a girl like you to land.*

2.

Made to wait in the front parlor, V hears the sheriff's engine disappear into the distance, feels the loss of that kind stranger tear at her young heart. The last hope she had to run for home, and now he's gone. *Wait,* she calls, rushing toward the doorway—

3.

You take your seat now, missy. We follow rules here.

4.

First, there are the necessary formalities of commitment to complete. Questions every girl must answer: name, address, employer, occupation, school, grade, special talents (dancing/singing), venereal conditions, intimate relations, with whom, and when, and where, conception date and place, name of the father—

Here V is forced again to tell the tale of that relation: How she met a man named Sammy K at the Cascade Club. How she'd heard that he was sick. How she'd gone to see him at the Curtis with a bowl of onion soup she hoped might help. February. She can't recall a date, but she's certain there was snow. *Yes, once. It wasn't more than once.* The hotel room at the Curtis? *Second or third floor,* V isn't sure. In town on a visit from St. Louis? Is V certain he's not local?

I'm sure, V lies again.

But a Jew, you're sure of that?

I am, V says, doling out the one truth Mr. C wanted V to tell.

5.

Don't start with the waterworks. The time for tears has passed.

6.

How shall we leave V on that first day?

Settled into the school's Higbee Hospital? A receiving ward of fourteen rooms, a sun porch, where V will live in isolation, quarantined for two long weeks, alone.

Or shall we leave her giving up her own clothes for the single dress and underwear the Home School first provides?

Or on the table with her bare feet in the stirrups? A strange man's hurried fingers tunneling through V. A delinquent girl about to be reformed.

[In a file built on fragments why pause at **Sammy K** ?
Or suspect it was a name Mr. C suggested,
or one young V invented on her own?
Sammy K,
V's answer to the carnal knowledge question,
the man the county hoped to charge.
An adjudication of paternity
that came to a dead end.
Case opened and abandoned
in the years that V was held.
"Father can't be found."
Why imagine Mr. C—
V's designated **"special friend"** —
when we have Sammy K?
A man who curiously mirrors Mr. C
in every way except St. Louis:
Nightclub manager, thirty-five, Jewish.
In a fiction built on fiction why doubt
V's own account of June's conception?

Intuition?
Or the caution against telling
I carry in my blood?]

Quarantine: Reception Wing

There is nothing V can give the other girls. No disease, no contraband. She only owns a regulation comb and toothbrush now. Still, she's contained in isolation like a germ. Subjected to their interviews and tests: Mantoux, Wassermann, vaginal smear, psychological, educational, achievement. A thorough investigation to ensure V is classified correctly.

Bed, table, dresser, chair. This is all V has for comfort now. A land of green and girls outside her window. The distant hum of inmates just like V. Footsteps in the hallway. The sealed jar of Higbee Hospital closed tight around V's brain.

At night, a lightning storm foreshadows Hell. V could die alone in these moist sheets. Die of want and terror. Die before this baby's even born.

And where is Em right now? Her hand in Lu's, two girls running from police like it's a lark. Mr. C closing up the Cascade Club, wiping a damp towel across the bar, or fingering V's button in the pocket of his pants. Mr. C dreaming of his V, his Little Fox, his Venus. His private, perfect dancer.

Another girl is dancing for him now.

In the morning, Higbee Hospital glares bright and disinfectant clean, and V can hear her mother's voice whisper from the walls.

Case Study

1.

V blinks out of isolation, startled by a sky suddenly silver; the solitary weeks a wool hood over her head. She has a face, a footprint, which means she must be real. She can still recite the streets of Minneapolis: Aldrich Avenue through Zenith. The states: Alabama, Arizona, Arkansas, etc. "The Raven." *Once upon a midnight dreary*. Her times tables through twelve. One-hundred-twenty-seven songs from start to finish. (A secret tally on the white page in her brain).

Two-thousand-thirty-six: the days that she has left to play their prisoner. Two-thousand-thirty-six.

In four more weeks, classified, case-studied, assigned the proper cottage, V will learn exactly who she is.

2.

Freed from quarantine, the fundamentals of V's training—homemaking and domestic service—must begin at once. Thus, V is on her knees waxing the glassy halls of Higbee Hospital; a daily exercise the school doctor recommends for pregnant girls.

3.

Evenings, V works the kitchen sink with loud Louise and Dixie from St. Paul, sweet Patrice from Minneapolis—Washburn High. Younger girls: Tough Toots who just turned twelve. Little Hazel only nine. Little Hazel with her frizzy pearl-white curls and pink-rimmed eyes, the tiny elfin girl who begs to sort the flatware. The best job in the kitchen and the big girls let her have it. Little Hazel who let her uncle touch her where he shouldn't. She knows better now, but can't go home. Her uncle plows her family's fields; Hazel doesn't.

You can be our Shirley Temple, V offers, to be kind. *Our own Baby Burlesk.* Once V wished to be that cute. That petulant and pouty. A Glad-Rags-to-Riches girl like charming Shirley.

If Shirley Temple let her uncle dirty her, Dixie says, disgusted. *But a rich girl in the pictures wouldn't do that.*

[Here I turn to other fragments:
The white space of statistics, of facts and forms,
of incomplete reports
the school submitted to the state.
Of some years that weren't V's years, but still—
a handwritten school ledger of minutia.
Tiny clues to V's lost story,
June's lost story,
suddenly the stories of thousands of lost girls.]

STATISTICS FOR THE FISCAL YEAR
ENDED JUNE 30, 1936

Offense Against Society

Bigamy	
Drunkenness	
Disorderly Conduct	1
Vagrancy	
Incorrigibility	10
Truancy	3
Immorality	79
All others in this class	1

Age

8 years	
9 years	1
10 years	1
11 years	
12 years	
13 years	2
14 years	13
15 years	21
16 years	22
17 years	32
18 years	9
19 years	1

—Minnesota Home School for Girls at Sauk Centre,
"Report to Minnesota State Board of Control," June 30, 1936

Girls in Institution on June 30, 1937 by Race:

White	247
Negro	7
Mexican	1
Indian	25
Other	1
Total	281

—Handbook of American Institutions for Delinquent Juveniles,
Vol. 1: West North Central States, 1938

[And this in the context of the 1930 and 1940 censuses, where 99.2% of the Minnesota population was identified as white.]

"The proportion committed until 21 years old was exceptionally large for males committed for delinquency and females committed for sex offenses immorality and sex delinquency—"

—Juvenile Delinquents in Public Institutions, 1933

"Because such a large proportion of the girls are sex delinquents. . . "

—*Minnesota Home School for Girls at Sauk Centre,*
"Report to Minnesota State Board of Control," June 30, 1936

[HOW TO BECOME A SEX DELINQUENT

This is difficult to accomplish on your own. An ordinary girl may need some help. Particularly young. Most frequently a sex delinquent girl will need a boy, an older neighbor who can rape her when she's twelve. Or a cousin who can take her in the closet, gag her mouth, make her hold his thing. A brother visiting her bed is helpful, too. Beyond these boys, perhaps a lucky girl will have a man. A father, uncle, stranger, a man who knows a secret game that they can play. First, the sex delinquent girl sits on his lap. This can start as young as one or two. That game isn't really fun, but the sex delinquent girl will never say so. Or maybe she's fifteen and never touched, but she wants to be in pictures. She's a girl who sings in choir, a girl who dances with her sisters and her friends. That girl must learn burlesque. Burlesque is where the money is right now. Men like to see a nearly naked young girl dance. Men like to imagine. The sex delinquent girl knows how to help a man imagine, the more a man imagines the more money she can make. Money feeds a sex delinquent girl. A sex delinquent girl is often hungry. Or her family's going hungry. Or she needs a place to sleep. Kind men can sell these sex delinquent girls. A sex delinquent girl must love adventure. A sex delinquent girl is sick. A sex delinquent girl puts all our men at risk. Boys and men. We must remove that girl. A sex delinquent girl can be reformed through housework. Do you wish to be a nanny or a maid? Answer yes. A sex delinquent girl will always answer yes.]

Assignment

After six weeks at Higbee Hospital, six weeks of inquisition while V kept the building clean, kept the oak floors gleaming with buffed wax, her case study is complete.

Classification: Expectant Mother.

Assignment: First Cottage, Fairview Colony. A cluster of five cottages for the pregnant, and the feeble-minded girls.

A place where troubled V will learn to find contentment in the home. Will learn to create a home for others. An aptitude that V and every other sentenced girl still lacks.

[Did you create a home at fifteen?]

V should pack her comb and toothbrush. Strip her bed. Leave the hospital without a long good-bye. It's best for girls to go without a fuss. The friends that she made here—Little Hazel, Sweet Patrice, Tough Toots—V may never know those girls again. Once assigned, communication between cottages is banned.

The girls in First Cottage, Fairview Colony—V shouldn't discount the feeble-minded—those girls will be her family unit now.

You've performed well in reception, Mrs. Lawson says. *The advisor finds you bright enough, but quite naïve. Star-struck like so many troubled girls. Claiming entertainment skills for which you haven't trained. Talents you clearly don't possess.*

I won the city solo contest, V would like to say, but she sits silent. Nine thousand people heard me sing in Minneapolis. Before my father died, he cleaned Lyndale Dance studio on Sundays for my lessons. Later, I had to learn routines by watching through the window, or I memorized dance numbers from movies, but at least I learned to dance.

But bright V doesn't speak. The little that she owns she isn't giving to this woman. The As she earned in elementary. The sixth-grade school operetta where they cast V as the lead. The selected soloist on Flag Day. V able to earn money for a song. So talented, she was discovered on the street and transformed into a star. Mr. C always proud of Little Fox. V, the shining star he knew she would be. That stole across her shoulders, the tips, the gifts from grateful customers, the thrill of their applause. Her dreams of Hollywood or Broadway.

Okay. V manages a shrug to show she doesn't care what Mrs. Lawson or the other staff might think. *I'll pack my toothbrush for First Cottage.*

First Cottage, where she'll train to clean and sew and launder for proper families when paroled.

The Weight of
Fairview Colony

The weight of girls. The weight of babies, secrets, shame. Amniotic fluid. The weight of want. The weight of rage. The weight of fieldwork and laundry. The weight of shovels, hoes, and spades. The weight of homesick, lovesick, lifesick, rising in V's gut. The weight of safe. The weight of fog through which the feeble-minded wander. Lost? Insane? No one ever says.

The dim girls bleed and bleed. The pregnant girls swell with salt and milk.

At night the fat girls lumber up the stairs, bears, bearing the weight of what they've done, and all they must do next.

[Does V vomit day and night as I once did,
from conception through delivery?
Vomit ceaselessly as June did with her first child?

My mother's mother always silent on the subject.
Never a single story of her pregnancy with June.
Of newborn June.
What she said to all our questions: *I really don't remember.*
And she didn't.

Family amnesia of adoption.
Of maternity. Of birth.
Amnesia of our history, and so I must invent.]

Early Days Fairview Colony: First Cottage

This is how V's days are measured here.

Hot nights of fitful sleep. On one close wall of V's cramped room, the movie of her dancing at the Cascade. On the other, a filthy sweat-soaked girl shovels dirt out in the sun.

Beyond this night-locked cottage, V is trapped by lake and pine and field with only one road for escape. That much V has learned already—how the brave girls try to run, how hard it is to hide among the ordinary now. A pregnant girl hitching in a homely state school dress. Regulation ankle boots with an X carved into each sole so girls are found. Men will hunt for V and bring her back.

V needs her child skin to harden here, needs another layer between what was and is—the six years still ahead she has to serve. Instead she lies here open as a peach soft in the center. The dark pit of her heart a small, black stone.

None of this will ever leave V's room—her 5:00 a.m. remorse, the silent movies she watches on her walls.

Among the matron, the officers, and staff in V's first cottage, she already has to be their street-tough tramp. The city girl who traded songs for fame and money. The star-struck girl who chased the nightlife and got what she deserved.

What all the girls deserve.

It's too late to beg God's mercy, too late to change the version of a life already lost.

Her day begins at 6:00 a.m., and so she goes—

"The general work of the institution, including the care of the gardens and poultry raising, but not heavy farm work, is done by the girls. However . . . there is a definite emphasis upon the training value of all assignments and it cannot be said that the labor of the girls is exploited."

—Handbook of American Institutions for Delinquent Juveniles,
Vol. 1: West North Central States, 1938

DAILY SCHEDULE
6:00 a.m.—Arise
7:00-9:00 a.m.—Breakfast, house cleaning duties, etc.
9:00-12:00 a.m.—School or assignments
12:00 Noon—Dinner
2:00-4:00 p.m.—School or assignments
4:00-6:00 p.m.—Recreation
6:00-7:15 p.m.—Supper
7:15-8:00 p.m.—Study hour
8:00-8:30 p.m.—Preparation for bed
8:30 p.m.—Bed

—Handbook of American Institutions for Delinquent Juveniles,
Vol. 1: West North Central States, 1938

A Group of Girls Outside Pioneer Cottage,
Minnesota Home School for Girls at Sauk Centre, ca. 1930

Maintenance

Every girl works maintenance in summer. Once her baby's born late October, V will go to school, but now this first hot June, she joins the pregnant and the dim, toiling in the garden for their food.

Always on her knees now, V plucks the rocks and weeds and worms to clear the soil, works the rows of lettuce, carrots, turnips, potatoes, zucchini, radishes, and beets. When the vegetables are ripe, girls will can them in the kitchen, storing up the pantry for the winter months ahead. All training V will need when she's paroled.

But V's a girl from Minneapolis, an apartment girl, a girl who never had to till the earth to eat. Summers she earned money tending toddlers on her street or selling kisses to the boys at Bryant Square. She'd sell a kiss again to get out of this garden. Once, a summer day could drift forever, rope swings and Ziegfeld paper dolls with Em, hide and seek out in the alley, doorbell ditch until the night filled up with stars. Before her mother took that husband, all before—

Beside V in the dirt, the girl Giselle—Gazelle the others call her— listens to V's stories, tells V that she will teach her how to run. Gazelle's escaped three times, but now she's pregnant. The week that she gives birth she'll bolt again. V dries her face with her damp sleeve, fights off the thick mosquitos, imagines fierce Gazelle running through the forest, crossing the border to Ontario with her handsome Northwoods hunter. Canada. A foreign country where a runaway lives free. She'll draw a map for V, meet her up in Winnipeg when V decides to run.

In the afternoon a rainstorm brings them in to mop the cottage. Gazelle again kneeling beside V—her sun-white hair cut jagged to her head, a punishment, but they can't break Gazelle—whispers all the ways a girl can run: Leap out an open window. Climb the low branch over the porch when the matron is asleep. Disappear in the darkness on the way to milk the cows.

Don't let your heart break here, Gazelle tells V, the baby in her belly arriving in late August, her runner's legs lean and strong, and ready for the world.

Recreation Hour

They pass it on the screened-in porch with a puzzle: V, the strong Gazelle, Tress with the beautiful black braids, Bun whose plump, plain face swells up like dough.

Secret names they've traded for Giselle, Therese, Bonita. Names the cottage staff can't learn or they'll be locked in isolation.

V takes the name of Foxy—Foxy for her ginger curls, the clever way she cons the officers, her schemes to beat the rules. Foxy for the girl she has become.

While the pregnant and the dim huddle at the radio for a chance to hear the dreary Philharmonic, Foxy and the Dames pretend to reconstruct an ancient mother-daughter puzzle Bun found on the shelf. A puzzle of propriety so old it reeks of must: a white-dressed, ribboned daughter with her arms around her mother. *You can bet this won't be me,* Foxy says, holding back the sudden urge to sweep the mildewed pieces to the floor.

Hell no, Gazelle agrees.

But the puzzle isn't all they're doing here. In gossip cloaked by scratchy violin, Bun laments the slop work in the pig-pen she's been assigned this month. She whispers how she bolted last November with a blanket and a sled, made it to Mankato where a butcher in an alley forced Bun to you-know-what. Now she's ruined for the future, a whale of a girl.

Tress tells how she was ravished, too. Ravished, the word the judge used at her hearing, like a thing a man could eat. Ravished by a boarder at a house her mother cleaned. The boarder grabbed Tress by the braid and gagged her mouth. Tress yanks her inky braid to prove the point.

Only Foxy and Gazelle will speak of love. How much they miss their men. Gazelle's beau a rugged hunting guide she met up near Bemidji on the run. She'd hid happy in his shack until a neighbor told the cops.

Stories that they've told and told again, hoarded like the silver from a country that they've lost. Pasts they're forbidden from disclosing, so they do.

Well, Mr. C was thirty-five, V brags. *A gangster with a gun.* She can be their Bonnie Parker without a trail of dead. *I was dancing down on Hennepin the day I was discovered. Strangers walking down the street would pay to see me dance.*

Burlesque? Bun asks, wide-eyed.

A showgirl, V corrects. *An entertainer. But, of course, I did it all.* Foxy is their daring, city star from Minneapolis, a girl who lived the dark side of downtown. *I wish that I could perform a number for you now.*

Me too, Gazelle says in a whisper.

Then her fingers are on V's, reaching for a corner of the mother's clean white blouse.

[Reform. To recreate, to change, to improve things for the better, to eradicate all defects, to break, to crack, to put together from the pieces, to reshape, remold, to modify, get straight, to convert, amend, revamp, to revise, restore, repair, to make something out of nothing, to fracture, to improve, to renovate, rework, to damage or destroy, to correct, resolve, to invent, to ameliorate, refine, to upgrade, to restructure, rearrange, to remedy, redeem. Reform V. Reform her pieces into story. To re-form what I have left.]

Magazines
such as
the following
may be included in the list
of reading for girls;

Post, *McCall's*, *Delineator*,
Pictorial Review,
Ladies' Home Journal,
American,
and *Woman's Home Companion*
depending on content.

No movie magazines may be included.

The *Christian Science Monitor*
is available to girls in each cottage

but they are not allowed
to read

the other daily papers.

     —*"Instructions for New Employee Training; Juvenile Institutions,*
Sauk Centre," 1937. Reprinted in the Handbook of American Institutions
for Delinquent Juveniles, Vol. 1: West North Central States, 1938

The First to Go

The baby Bun didn't want dies in the night. The other girls asleep, Bun alone at Higbee Hospital delivering the dead.

Fragment. Finger. Foot.

When Bun wakes, the day nurse warns her not to wallow. *It's for the best,* she says. *What good is another girl like this?*

True, Bun should be relieved, but instead she feels like something has been stolen, a body of her body gone against her will.

The girls dig a secret grave out in the garden. Pretend to bury May among the radishes. (The Dames have made a pact to name their babies after months.) A cut of Tress's braid. A thumb prick of Bun's blood. A tiny cross Bun fashioned from stolen thread and sticks. Two pieces of the mother-daughter puzzle V stole from the box. No one can complete it now, with Bun's poor daughter dead.

At least she's free, Foxy offers as their prayer. *Better dead than here, God rest her soul.*

Go up to the sky now, little bird, Gazelle adds gently.

I'll see you at the rapture, May, Bun says to the dirt. Her lips against the land like May can hear.

[And where is dead May really?

Buried in a place that Bun can't visit.

May, an unmarked grave
in a local farmer's field.
Another state school secret
effectively erased under waist-high grass
and weeds.

May
another never-happened baby
a stranger
laid to rest.]

Transfer One

Tonight, before the matron transfers Bun to General Population, the four Dames make a vow to stay Blood Sisters, tough girls who won't be tamed.

The punishments ahead—cold baths and slaps, isolation, weeks of bread and water, hair shaved down to the scalp—all of that will prove how hard they are.

Gazelle slips the stolen scissors from her hem, carves a hurried D into Bun's arm. Another into Tress's. Foxy next, and Foxy doesn't flinch.

Finished, Gazelle asks Bun to do the honor, and she does.

Leave your mark on me, she says. *I'll miss you.*

Now all of them wear D.

D for Dames.

Delinquent.

Deviant.

Demented.

Depraved.

Degenerate.

Despondent. They won't see Bun again.

I guess I'll see you on the hard road, Bun says bravely.

Or the low road, Foxy laughs.

On the dark side, Tress says, blinking back bright tears.

Don't let them break you, babe, Gazelle says, pressing a kiss to Bun's plump cheek. They can lock Gazelle up for that last kiss, she doesn't care.

Long live the Dames, Bun sobs, like she might break already.

The raw welt from her fresh D burning like a promise she can't keep, not alone in Van Cleve Cottage Two.

Correspondence

Every two weeks, V may write one letter to her family.

Every week, V's family may send one letter in return.

For V, the state provides the stamps.

All state school correspondence, written and received, is inspected by the officers because naturally V's welfare must come first.

There is no truth that censored V can tell. An honest letter from her time will never be discovered. *I'm getting by just fine,* she writes her mother. *The girls here sure can cook. We get a nice breeze off the lake.*

One wrong word to Minneapolis, and her mail privileges will be lost.

The Letter V Can't Write or Send, and So She Doesn't

August 3, 1936

Dear Em,

Are you still running free? How'd I end up here, and a girl like you still loose? I can't really write to you because we had to quit all friends. Are you best friends with Lu now? Do you ever think of me? That summer we first smoked in the cattails near the creek? A pack of cigarettes you swiped from some old man. Or the time Danny Olson took up with that tramp, and we broke his bedroom window. Hahaha.

This summer I'm just working in the dirt. Beetles, worms, and bugs. Those fuzzy baby caterpillars we'd let crawl along our skin. I'm fat. I look just like a walrus. Don't tell Mr. C I'm fat, or he won't love me anymore.

Do you still see Mr. C? Does he have another girl? Please write and tell me NO. If he doesn't, tell him V is still his girl. Tell him his secret's safe with me until I die. (He'll know what you mean.) Please write back quick and tell me how he is.

Is the beach crowded with the kids? Remember summer nights when we laid a blanket on the sand and slept there to stay cool? Or swam in-you-know-what at Cedar Lake? It's so damn hot here I can't sleep; I only sweat. I bet you've found a new friend with me gone. Ever hear my name, or am I just the girl sent off to the state school? Lu is probably happy to have you to herself.

I can't tell you how it is here, unless you're interested in laundry, canning, scrubbing, ironing, and waxing. (I know for sure YOU AREN'T.) They're training us to keep house for the rich. Not me, I've still got my heart set on Broadway. Maybe you'll run with me to New York? No matter what they say, I'm not scrubbing floors when I get sprung.

We've got a small gang called the Dames, four that's down to three. The Dames are swell, the toughest in the bunch. I'm a tough girl, too. Did you think that I stayed sweet? Well, not for long. The pen isn't the adventure you liked to make-believe.

Keep those nasty boys away, or you'll end up like I did. On the other hand, I'd like to have you here.

> Yours until Niagara Falls,
> Your Forgotten Best Friend,
> Eileen Sideways (aka V)

P.S. If you walk by the Cascade, check the posters on the door. Let me know who's singing for him now.

[And eighteen years beyond Miss Fannie French Morse's rousing 1919 speech, the Minnesota Home School for Girls at Sauk Centre holds true to her bright dream. America's ambitions for reformed girls remarkably consistent.]

"Because the girls of today become the wives and mothers of tomorrow, the emphasis in training in the school is placed upon home making and home management."

—*Minnesota Home School for Girls at Sauk Centre,*
"Report to Minnesota State Board of Control," June 30, 1936

The Wives and Mothers of Tomorrow

Like every other prisoner, pregnant V survives on dreams. First, the baby miraculously gone. Then, on a highway white with sunshine, Mr. C suddenly appears, calls V to his Ford and they escape, start over in New York where V's a star. The law won't ever find V in New York.

At eighteen, without anyone's permission, V will be his lawful wife. She sees their fancy brick apartment, the spire of the Empire State Building just out their bedroom window, their rumpled bed, the marble basin she wipes clean of his black whiskers, the glass table where she serves him two poached eggs. White roses on the table, Mr. C bought as a gift. Mr. C dressed in his classic tie and emerald cufflinks, a starched white shirt that V knows how to mend and launder now. Mr. C happy to be far from Minnesota with his star.

The baby gone.

The baby always gone.

The First Escape

Baby August eight days old, Gazelle is gone.

V can't say how or where. The windows locked at night; cottage doors bolted before dinner. Somehow Gazelle has made her way across the miles of open field, hiding in the corn, moving between clusters of thick trees like a coyote.

The things she's left for V: Her courage. Proof V can escape. A stolen key behind the puzzle V will never find. Baby August. Without a mother to attend him, he's the school's problem now.

August thrashing at the bottle, squalling for the breast. The school will only keep a baby if the mother is retrieved, otherwise the state will find a proper home. They can't afford to feed a lost girl's son.

V tries to force the nipple in his mouth to make him drink, to stop his desperate crying, which is more than V can bear. If it wasn't for Gazelle, she'd kill him now.

Don't cry, she pleads in whispers. Gazelle would want her son to eat. Gazelle, running toward a forest where she'll sleep under pine and spruce. Forest after forest, living off farmers' vegetables and berries, moving in the darkness, hiding in the day. A method she taught V, so V can follow. Gazelle, a girl at home with brothers, if her brothers were the trees. Her muscles strong and angry, just like August's.

Your mother isn't coming, V whispers to his cheek. *And she wouldn't want us crying; she'd want us to be strong.*

Be strong now, she repeats. Then finally he is latching on the bottle, guzzling toward strength in V's reluctant arms. August, already no one's baby; Gazelle running for her life.

Third Trimester

At first it was a pale shrimp curled pink inside V's belly, now it is a mammal the size of a small cat. V feels its gnawing paws claw at her ribs, feels the burrow of its skull between her legs, a thrashing angry animal fighting at the cave where it's been kept.

Assigned a second day of harvest, V's back bent and aching from the weight. Palms blistered from the work, she prays for death to take them both. The dead cat buried in a hatbox, the two of them finally cool beside V's father in the dirt. *Hello, hon, you're here! Why don't you sing a song for Daddy?*

Mr. C visiting their graves to weep with guilt.

Let him weep.

At night the cemetery watchman passes with a lantern, pauses at V's grave to read the dead girl's name and date. Too young, he thinks. (V imagines this the headline in the story of her life. Or carved into a marble gravestone Mr. C will buy. Didn't she keep his secret? Didn't she end up here?)

Too Young, the watchman reads, but he moves on.

Compliance

Once Gazelle and Bun are gone, once Tress betrays their pact and names her baby George, once the power of the Dames has disappeared, V decides to feign compliance, knits like other girls in Recreation, endures their constant chatter—how skinny they once were, how much they miss their figures—another version of the babble V and Em abhorred at junior high. Why V had to quit the Glee Club. The after-school choir. ("Under the supervision of the school personnel, they learn to behave like average girls.") V doesn't want to be an average girl. Average is a rock along the road. Potato dull. A brain as blank as squash. As dreary as V lives now, she might as well be dead. Knit one, purl two.

But bathing in the tub or brushing out her hair before the mirror at the sink, V tells herself she's someone special still: a girl with secret talents, a girl imprisoned in a tower like Rapunzel. A girl destined to be greater than these yellow boots she's knitting for the birth.

Visitation Sunday,
September 1936

The first time Mr. C arrives he's V's thoughtful "Cousin Harold," chauffeuring V's sisters in his beautiful black Ford. (A secret hint smart V is quick to catch—Cousin Harold doesn't drive.) Cousin Harold delivering V's beloved older sisters: Lydia and Rose. (Ida far away with Baby Wesley in Cheyenne.) Proper Lydia pregnant just like V, but so much prettier in a Swiss dot dress their mother made last week. Sweet Rose in V's old skirt. She's home now from Milwaukee, and secretly divorced. A barely one-year marriage that Rose has managed to erase.

Clean slate, Rose smiles. *Mother says five years from now, no one will remember.* Sweet Rose always on the bright side. *I'm home with Mom and Ray; sleeping in your room.*

V so shocked to see her sisters that she cries. *I can't believe you're here,* she says, embarrassed by her great balloon of belly, her greasy pimpled forehead, her cracked hands calloused from the work.

Thanks to Cousin Harold, Rose says with a wink. *He's parked down the road with all the other men.* Too far away for V to even steal a glimpse. Female family members only at the school.

And Mother? V asks, worried. *She didn't want to visit, too?*

Worn thin, like always, Lydia says, taking in the Morse Hall fancy parlor where the girls may greet their guests. Gleaming hard wood floors. Vases of fresh flowers the girls cut and arranged. *You know how hard she works. And all your troubles haven't helped her health.*

Cousin Harold says he's sorry he can't see you, Rose says to change the subject. *But he sent you a few things.* She hands V a fancy Dayton's bag of tissue-papered gifts: silk stockings, lemon drops, an expensive ruby pin. Nothing V can wear or eat or keep and so the bag goes back to Rose.

I can't, she says, more tears hot on her cheeks.

Oh sweet little V, Rose soothes, twisting V's limp hair into a curl, wiping off V's tears with her soft thumb. *Cousin Harold hopes you're singing. Is radio allowed? Have you heard Amateur Hour? Cousin Harold says you'll be singing on that someday, and you'll win. He says he's never seen such talent. Never once. And I guess he's a good judge—*

He did? V asks, unsure of fact or fiction. Mr. C, a family stranger, told all of that to Rose?

Ah yes, dear Cousin Harold. Proper Lydia's sharp sigh a scissor of suspicion. *Did you know he bought Mother a brand new Philco? A radio when she and Ray can barely make their rent? Does that make sense to you, V?*

V shakes her head. It doesn't. None of this makes sense. Her sisters' sudden visit. A radio from Mr. C. Did he go to her apartment? Tell her mother who he was? The owner of the Cascade? The man who named their daughter Little Fox? The father of this baby? V doubts he told them that. And then to drive her sisters—

He knew Mother would be lonely with V gone, Rose says, like all of Lydia's suspicions should end with those few words.

And is she? V dares, hoping for a yes. Does her mother truly miss V? Does she wish that V were home?

I just find his generosity— Lydia says, her hands on her round belly while she's staring hard at V's. *Well, don't you find it odd, V?*

I guess, V says. Wishing she could see her man of minor honor. Her man who kept his word.

[The inheritance of fiction.
Fiction as survival.]

"It cannot be said the labor of the girls is exploited."

—Handbook of American Institutions for Delinquent Juveniles,
Vol. 1: West North Central States, 1938

"Labor:

Persistent exertion of body or mind; bodily toil for the sake of gain or economic production; those engaged in such toil considered as a group or class;

Work or a task done or to be done; the product or result of toil; the process of childbirth.

To perform labor; exert one's power of body or mind; work; toil; to move with effort or difficulty; roll or pitch heavily as a ship; to be burdened, troubled, or distressed; to be in travail or childbirth."

—New Webster's Dictionary of the English Language, 1980

[Excerpted here from the rare gift that June bought me. College graduation. 1982.]

[EXAMPLES OF LABOR]

1. The girls' labor was undocumented.
2. To maintain the school, the farm, the fields, the girls' (unexploited) labor was required.
3. V went into labor this morning.
4. Will V's labor ever end?
5. V had a difficult labor.
6. The doctor rested from his labor.

A Difficult Labor

1.

The first pain hits V during laundry. V working the soap along the washboard leans against the metal tub and howls. A river of hot liquid rushes down her leg, pools like pee around her leather boots. November 3. Ten days overdue, but now this stubborn baby will be born.

2.

So much worse than V imagined. Could imagine. Could not.

3.

V has no words, just moments moving into moans. Wet washcloth on her forehead. A room at Higbee Hospital. A gag over her mouth to silence screams.

4.

Someone squeezing her small hand.

Someone scolding,
someone saying,
You'll survive.
You're not the first or last.

5.

Crushing waves of pain strangling V's abdomen and back. A boulder.
The baby is a giant boulder now.

6.

V just ninety pounds when this baby was conceived. Not even five-feet tall.

7.

Fifteen.

8.

Next time she'll think twice, the doctor says.

9.

Eighteen hours later V howls into the night, feels the boulder smash her pelvis, her tailbone, her back. *Push,* the doctor orders. *This baby isn't going to get here on its own.*

10.

Things inside V now:
Forceps. Scissors. Hands.
This baby.
This baby not wanting to be born.

11.

The animal of pain that is V's body. Living, breathing anguish V will not forget.

12.

Next time she will think twice.

13.

What she knows is finished.
Done.
Delivered.
The sound of someone crying with her now.
That thing.
That thing.

14.

A girl, the doctor says. *Another goddamn girl.*

15.

He rested from his labors.

Postpartum Dream One

In V's dream June is a cat, black-lashed and gray-bellied, mewing at V's breast, begging V for milk. June's a cat brought in a basket, a birthday gift from Mr. C, one V wishes to return, but she can't say it. Instead V climbs a tree, the gnarled low-limb oak at Loring Park. V finds a rope, ties a noose around June's neck. The cat's too quick. V cannot kill the cat.

Postpartum Dream Two

While V sleeps there is a ship docking in a harbor, and her mother new from Norway walking down the gangplank with a steamer trunk of custom clothes she's sewn for the rich.

A woman walks a lion on a leash. Another wears a twist of fox fur knotted at her neck. *We're in America,* one says, and they all laugh.

June trails like a tail attached to V's old coat, a foreign child frozen by some fear. *You're here,* a tall man says as he lifts June to his shoulder, points out the Foshay Tower, the courthouse clock, the Cascade Club. *She'll need a ticket in this country,* he tells V. *A ticket to the city.*

The Minneapolis skyline a dazzle of bright diamonds in the dark.

[REPARATION]

"In Minnesota, under a joint resolution adopted in July, 1918, by the State board of health and the board of control, hospitals and maternity homes must require their patients to nurse infants at the breast, as long as they remain under the care of the institution.

[. . .] It has been the experience of the association that the appeal to the un-married mother to nurse her baby at least for the minimum period of three months as a kind of reparation for having brought him into the world so handicapped is an almost unfailing argument."

—*Emma O. Lundberg,* Children of Illegitimate Birth and
Measures for Their Protection, *Bureau Publication No. 166,*
U.S. Department of Labor, Children's Bureau, 1926

[June.
A name that will be changed in two short years.

And yet I call her June here
in honor of that baby girl she was.]

How They Bond

From the dark crate of Higbee Hospital, the future is a pinhole of possibility, a tinfoil crown of someday V can't live without. June screams while V dips into a dream, spreads her arms wide into wings, flies back to fifteen, Mr. C, the Cascade Club. June, a squalling, angry infant enraged at V's hot breast. Nurse Kelly clasps June's neck, coos *shhh* and *shush* to make a show of patience, but June rears her stubborn head. V's milk a trick of poison June can't trust.

Let her know there's love, Nurse Kelly orders.

How? V asks, while Nurse Kelly shoves V's raw nipple in June's mouth.

After Birth

1.

V begs to leave like Esther. Esther, daughter of a banker and ready to go home. Baby birthed at Higbee Hospital, then gone. No baby in the nursery. Rich Esther leaving on an ordinary Wednesday. Esther in a new blue dress to hide what might have happened. Esther disappearing in a Cadillac, as if that baby boy were never born.

2.

So why can't V leave, too? Give the baby to a stranger? Because the Minnesota Resolution requires every baby born out of wedlock to be breast-fed. Requires everyone, but Esther. A lesson V must learn: mother's milk is best for these poor babies. The state can't afford to feed them all. *Next time you'll think twice.* V holds the angry baby to her breast, endures the excruciating latch, rooting June, June sucking, sucking, sucking, V's nipples cracked and bleeding, scabbed, milk leaking down her dress while she scrubs floors, breasts engorged, breast infection and a fever, a hot hard lump the doctor must massage, hot packs day and night until V's well, and still June feeds. Breasts put to proper use. Breasts for babies only. Babies only. V understands that now.

"Handle the baby as little as possible. Turn occasionally from side to side, feed it, change it, keep it warm, and let it alone; crying is absolutely essential to the development of good strong lungs. A baby should cry vigorously several times each day."

—William S. Sadler and Lena K. Sadler,
The Mother and Her Child, *1916*

Nursery Magic

1.

Slow as it unfolds, and unexpected. V's the only person that can make June's crying stop. June only calms for V, and V won't let June cry. June's wail is full of want that V knows well. The baby only asks for love; why not let her have it?

2.

So there is V swaying baby June until she calms. V singing *hush-a-bye,* and *rock-a-bye,* and "Tea for Two," even that strange Norwegian lullaby her mother used to sing. Old country words V doesn't really know and so she hums. V changing June's soaked diaper, cleaning June's chapped butt, V reeking of dried milk and spit, V warning all the officers—*That isn't how you hold her, rock her, burp her.* V the fierce new mother of a baby she didn't want.

3.

June blinks. June yawns. June smiles. June reaches for the rattle. June makes a fist around V's fingers, won't let go. June's eyes follow V. June listens. June settles at the sound of V's soft voice. June turns her head toward V. Dark-eyed June like Mr. C. A head of jet-black hair. June blows bubbles and she gurgles. June laughs. V teaches June to waltz; June loves to waltz. June holds up her head. June lifts up from her belly. June only likes to nuzzle in V's neck. June won't let the others hold her. She just won't. Day after stubborn day, June insisting on V's heart.

Our morning gone to research, June's hips aching from the stiff-backed wooden chair, her eyes exhausted from the harsh fluorescent light, still she refuses to quit, refuses to leave her state-held papers for even an hour to grab lunch.

You should eat, I urge, but June won't budge.

She's deep into the adoption papers now, dissecting every sentence, taking notes on every detail of her early missing years. Pausing at the mysteries: *Breastfed? I was breastfed for three months? I lived there as a baby? But then they took me? Doesn't that seem strange? Cruel, too?*

It does, I say, confounded by a detail it will take ten years to solve.

And look at this, June urges, her whisper verging on a tremble, except June doesn't cry. Not ever in my lifetime. *V wanted me, she did. It says so here:* **"V intends to keep her baby."**

Proof June needs to show me, a revelation in the papers June wants a witness to record. Gray-haired June suddenly that infant taken from V's arms. *Even at fifteen,* June says in awe, as if that one fact in the file is all we'd come to find.

First Christmas June

What V has for June today—a hand-sewn gingham rabbit, floppy eared, black whiskers stitched in thread, pearl buttons for the eyes; a bar of perfumed soap (V's gift from Ladies' Aid) that V will share; talcum powder from the matron; the knitted yellow boots; a winter land of icicled white trees, laced filigree frozen on the windows; Christmas morning silence; the gift of V's young love. V's promise of bright holidays ahead—how it will be once V is freed. Their someday tinseled tree; presents in bright paper; June ripping off the wrapping with surprise. Krumkake and pepperkaker, lutefisk and lefse; the perfect Christmas life V's precious girl deserves. A warm apartment rich with rømmegrøt and pine; V singing "Silent Night"; sweet Rose on the piano; June in a special velvet dress and shiny shoes; a restless night of Santa dreams. In the life V dreams for June, Santa always comes.

Babies at Minnesota Home School for Girls at Sauk Centre

[What They Will Be Called in June's Lifetime:
Bastard. Illegitimate. Adulterated. Unfortunate.
Baseborn. False and fake. Impure.
Misborn. Misbegotten.
Always misbegotten.
Irregular, ingenuine, a sham.
Damaged goods from the beginning.
Unworthy and unwanted.
Always damaged goods.]

Collect

Without warning, Rose and Mr. C come to "collect." Collect, as if V owes them a debt, and June is what they're taking in return.

June, this baby born from V's body, will be V's mother's baby now. V's mother and sweet Rose at home to help.

She'll be in good hands with your mother, Matron Turnblad says. *What better place than family for the child?*

Whose hands? Her mother's hands exhausted from the sewing? The second husband's filthy hands? V doesn't want that man to handle June. *She won't,* V says, clutching June against her chest. *June needs me.*

It's just until parole, Rose says, to reassure. *She'll be your girl again when you get out.*

V's first hearing will be April; June can't live without a mother for that long.

But Esther, V says to Matron Turnblad. An argument V's fought before, but she's prepared to fight again. V wants her chance at justice: she can raise this baby that she loves. V and Mr. C the true parents June deserves. (Mr. C outside at this minute, posing once again as Cousin Harold in the Ford. He can marry V. He must love V and June, or he wouldn't be waiting now.) *You let Esther leave. She didn't even keep her baby. I'll take good care of mine. You've seen it for yourself. June can't be without me. We've never been apart.*

V, Rose pleads. She doesn't want a scene here in the office.

I know it was their money, V says, a flood of fresh tears dripping from her cheeks to June's dark hair. *Baby, baby, baby,* V coos, swaying side to side. If V's father owned a bank, she'd be home now. *I can give you money.*

V, Rose says again. Her hand against June's leg; June rearing back. *June will be with family. And we'll bring her here as often as we can. Cousin Harold's promised—*

Good-hearted Rose always on V's side. Still, V detects new greed in Rose's eager, reaching hands. The rush to play new mother with her locked-up sister's child. Divorced Rose, without a baby, can play house now with June.

Say your last good-bye, V, Matron Turnblad orders.

Hush-a-bye, V sings. Mother ache, a pain she'll need to beat down to survive.

V looks into June's eyes, dark and wise and full of trust in V. What will she remember of V's love? All their days of stories. Secrets V has shared. June's fist around V's finger; June's fist around V's hair. Noses tip to tip. June sucking on V's cheek. *Hush little one,* V sings, kissing her own tears on June's damp head. *Baby, baby, baby.* It isn't quite a song. A song could end. This one V can sing until tomorrow.

That's enough, the Matron says, yanking June out of V's arms. June screaming for V now. Screaming June handed off to Rose. Rose jostling and bouncing to make the screaming stop.

Don't bounce! V screaming, too. *June hates to bounce.*

The matron shoving Rose out of the office, latching both locks on her door so V can't run. *You'll live to see worse,* the matron scolds. *You'll forget this in a week.*

I won't, V says, and here she tells the truth.

Attachment Theory: One

June screaming all the way to Minneapolis, frazzled Rose putting her finger in June's mouth. Mr. C saying, *Babies cry. Eventually they quit.* [Eventually June claims she cannot cry.] June screaming through tomorrow, and the next day, day after day of racking sobs no one can calm. June in V's old bedroom, crying in the crib that Cousin Harold bought at Sears. Bottles cold or warm, blankets tight or loose, diapers clean or dirty, rocking, walking, bouncing, nothing comforts June. V's seamstress mother taking June at midnight so Rose can get some sleep. Rose deadtired at the bakery, but glad to leave V's screaming baby at the sitter's down the hall. June never in Ray's care because Rose knows. [Or is that just wishful thinking?] Rose a failed mother standing at June's crib when it's V that June expects. Forever and forever and forever, it will be V that June has lost.

[Inexplicable to June,
but she cannot love her first-born,
or the ones that follow after
in the years before "the pill."

Any desperate, cash-strapped stranger,
June will pay to be our mother.
Lazy teenaged girls. Impatient widows.
The indifferent next-door neighbor saving for a car.
When my oldest sister turns six, June lets her take the job.

A heart of stone, June likes to tell us as a joke.
But exactly why she has it, June can't answer.
That question is the mystery of June.]

Losing June

What V needs now is a dress of mourning crepe. Stiff black. An onyx veil the color of June's eyes.

All V has learned to love—the smell of powdered skin, the sound of June's sweet jabber, the rush of June's milk surging through V's breasts—all of that is air.

V worships at the altar of lost things, her grief a second skin. A life of constant absence for which V can't prepare. Nothing in the world will be her own, except perhaps her sins. Every price she's made to pay, she pays, and pays again.

The life she leads from here—decent or depraved—nothing that V does will bring June back.

Early Lessons Cottage Six

V will live in Cottage Six until parole.

The matron with the spotted hands is mean.

Steal the wooden spools to crimp your hair.

Fast girls do things in private V might like.

Matron Klas smells like moldy cheese and mothballs.

Mary Conway plays the organ Sunday mornings for the service.

Mary Conway is the leader of the Crimps.

If you're captured on the lam they shave your head.

If you're captured on the lam then you'll be tubbed.

If you're captured on the lam you're in lock-up for two weeks.

Maybe for a month. Two months.

Bread and milk for meals.

At night you line your shoes outside the door.

Always hang your clothes or they'll be gone.

The matron does inspection.

The matron with the spotted hands is mean.

If Bonnie Hartman grips your wrist it means you're in.

Bonnie Hartman is the leader of the Hens.

A girl can't stand alone here and be safe.

A lone girl is a lamb.

V will need to choose a gang.

The matron with the spotted hands is mean.

View at Home School for Girls, Sauk Centre, Minn.

146

"**Rules, Regulations, and Disciplinary Policies**—[. . .] routine administration of discipline is left to the cottage mothers [. . .] There are no printed rules and regulations and it was stated that 'ordinary standards of conduct are the basis of discipline at the home school.'

Punishments—The various punishments include deprivation of privileges, confinement in a regular room, extra or unpleasant work assignments, corporeal punishment, cold tubbings, segregation, isolations, and delayed parole.

Corporal punishment, in the form of slapping is permitted but not encouraged."

—Handbook of American Institutions for Delinquent Juveniles,
Vol. 1: West North Central States, 1938

[AND ELSEWHERE OTHER GIRLS

Chillicothe, Tipton, Kearney, Beloit, Plankinton, Mitchellville, Hudson, Geneva, Lancaster, etc. etc. In 1936, young V was not alone. Girls stripped, whipped, laid naked on a desk while others watched. East and West and North and South. Home School, State School, Industrial Training School. State Home for Negro Girls. Schools for problem girls in every state. Girls sterilized against their will, the heyday of eugenics. All girls assigned to house work, farm work, ironing, and laundry. Cottage system as a family so incarceration feels like home.

Firm but loving matrons they call Mother. Schools with sympathetic understanding. Sincere devotion to the training of the immoral and incorrigible. (Of course, the sex problems with some girls cannot be stopped.) Every three months, one month, depends upon the school, visits from the family must be earned. Not here, but there. Dungeon. Hamper. Segregation cells in basements or hot attics. Windows barred with wood or iron. Ventilation adequate. (Not always.) In case of fire, the girls would not escape. Switch across the shoulders. Switch across the legs. School scaled down "to teach the retardation characteristic of these girls." Library Dewey decimal-ed and censored. Food palatable, or not. Waitress, sink girl, scrub girl. Every girl will get her chance to serve. No social worker, psychiatrist, psychologist. Spanking, slapping, shackled. Or were the shackled only boys? Strapped. Hair cut. Heads shaved. No dinner, no dessert.

Deprivation of entertainment, moving pictures, recreation, radio. No records of disciplinary action kept. Punishments at the staff's discretion. Always their discretion. The law is silent on this matter. The risk of girls going up in flames. Isolation, segregation, standing in a corner for a day.

Not here, but someplace else. Say Ireland, perhaps? The Magdalene's. Their laundries.

Never in Missouri, Kansas, Minnesota, New York, Massachusetts, California, and every other state.

Never in America. Not us.]

"This training is given to all girls in connection with the regular maintenance work . . . there is no question of 'cottage training' being a euphemism for 'getting institutional work done.'"

"Care of own room and personal sewing	1 month
Room, sewing and halls	1 month
Girls' bathroom	1 month
Stairs	1 month
Living room	1 month
Lower hall	1 month
Officers' room service	2 months

When the above schedule has been completed to the satisfaction of the house mother, and the assistant superintendent, the girls are transferred to the dining room and kitchen supervisor to complete the following assignments:

First sink work	1 month
Second sink work	1 month
Basement	1 month
Laundry	1 month
Junior waitress	1 month
Junior cook	1 month
Senior cook	2 months
Senior waitress	2 months

While serving as senior waitress each girl is required to make her outfit of parole clothing including two work dresses, two afternoon prints, and a silk dress."

"There is no direct program of character education, it being considered that all activities have character forming as their main objective."

—Handbook of American Institutions for Delinquent Juveniles, Vol. 1: West North Central States, 1938

Beyond Motherhood

V has grown solid. Grown strong enough to split the birch and oak, haul it to the fire, and burn whatever love of June is left. Hard work. The matron's answer to all grief. The lost babies no more than summer frogs the girls found in the forest. Pets the girls couldn't keep. V imagines her family's mailbox on Emerson filled with all her secret *Missing You's* for June, scribbled notes the school won't let V send. Maybe a red ringlet of V's hair. Her mother scent held tight in June's small hand. V cracks the ax again against the birch, imagines the school disappearing. The dining room of girls. The grimy sink. Anything to make this long day done. Imagines her ax against the matron's skull. That bitch boss who ripped June from V's strong arms, whose gravel voice was grit against V's tender nerves. That bitch. V slams the ax a third time as a wish. How close V comes to murder—the silver second between another's life and death—how close V comes to knowing she could kill.

Every Two Weeks

V waits for news of June: how many teeth, what new words June can say—just once V wants to hear her daughter's voice—but suddenly, Rose's tales of peek-a-boo and patty-cake are gone. Now, the only news of June they write is "fine."

Fine could be Sally, Susan, Amy, Mary Ann, or Jeanne. Fine is any baby ever born.

V knows the inmates' missing babies can't be mentioned at the school; perhaps the families are forbidden from speaking of them, too. Out of sight so out of mind, the staff is quick to say. Cruel silence. But everything is cruel.

Instead, Rose sends V empty updates: A red formal Mother made for Mrs. Winton. Lydia's Peter sick with sniffles for two weeks. Ray saw a downtown doctor for his hip. (V doesn't want to hear a word of Ray.) Ida pregnant with her second in Cheyenne.

Time flies, Rose likes to write, and yet it doesn't.

Hank came by for dinner twice last week. He seems sweet enough on me, but who can tell? He's working at the brake shop now on Portland. The days are gray. I imagine it's the same there in Sauk Centre. Maybe we'll visit for your birthday, if Cousin Harold's free. Poor Hank's too broke to buy a car yet, but he will.

June is a happy girl as always.

Two weeks, V waits for this? One short page of nothing. They can burn it in the trash for all she cares. The staff's already read it; it's been censored and approved.

Have you finished? Mrs. Klas asks, holding out her hand. Every piece of V belongs to someone else.

V drops the letter on the desk and turns to leave without asking Mrs. Klas first for permission. A serious infraction, but V's too enraged to care.

Four weeks for your insolence, Mrs. Klas says, locking V's dull letter in the drawer. *I'll hold onto your mail until your attitude improves.*

You go ahead, V says.

Or better yet, six weeks, Mrs. Klas says to V's stiff back. *And they're not to write of romance. Your sister should know that.*

[EVIDENCE OF V: JULY 1975, WYOMING

Imagine someone is a secret.
Imagine all these years not knowing someone lived.
Imagine me, at sixteen on a visit to Cheyenne,
staring at a photo of a strange girl and asking who *she* is.

She, my great-aunt Ida says,
is our youngest sister, V.

V?

How could there be a sister I didn't know?
A missing girl
Grandma Rose has never mentioned to me once?
In every tale of her childhood only her two devoted sisters,
Lydia and Ida,
that pair of strong Norwegian women
I've loved well.

V? I ask again, confused. *Where is she?*

Never mind all that, Great Aunt Ida says too quickly,
closing the cover on that history without another word.]

"Each girl is automatically interviewed by the Board of Control at the end of one year in the school. Matron and housekeeper will be asked for their recommendation on her cottage training, work, work habits, and character.

Girl should have clean and fairly new dress when she appears for her interview. Dress preferably made by herself."

—"Instructions; Sauk Centre Home School." Reprinted in the
Handbook of American Institutions for Delinquent Juveniles,
Vol. 1: West North Central States, 1938

Interview Board of Control

For the daughter of a seamstress, V's sewing is substandard. The Board should check her buttons, take one look at that hem. *Obviously, she didn't dress to impress.* (Except V did; she worked hard to sew this modest day dress for the Board.)

Of course, her first months at Fairview Colony can't be wholly counted toward parole. Those poor pregnant girls are limited in all that they must learn. So busy with their babies in the nursery, and V was meddlesome with hers. Arguing with officers and staff about the child. Coddling. An unnatural attachment to the infant frequently reported by the staff. It's right there in her records. Not in the best interest of the child.

V's had four months in Cottage Six to pass personal sewing, and she hasn't. She's sloppy and impatient with a tendency to rush. She'll need better skills to do the sewing for the school. During her first two months with poultry, eggs were left behind. Her attitude is reckless; she forces staff to punish her, she does. And she's attracted to the worst sex delinquent girls, still too eager to keep company with trouble. Betty Carter. Audra Lamb, who twice tried to escape. So far there's no sign that V will finish training in a year. Fifteen months would be more likely. And, of course there is the question of the missing father that V named. That Jewish nightclub manager she supposedly brought soup. The Women's Bureau hasn't found him yet. Would V like to change her story?

No, she wouldn't.

It may be another fifteen months before the girl is ready, the Board leader declares.

Fifteen months? V shrieks like she's insane. She claws deep lines along each cheek, pulls her perfect hair. Let them lock her up; ship her off to the asylum. Other inmates went insane just to get transferred. *My baby needs her mother. Every baby does. I can't train another fifteen months.*

Stop with the hysterics, the matron says, unmoved. She doesn't even glance in V's direction. *This one is a hard case,* she says coldly to the Board. *Regardless, we intend to persevere.*

Escape

When Audra runs in May, V wakes to a shadow in her doorway, wakes to livid Mrs. Klas barking V from bed. *Get up,* she shouts, and V joins the line of blinking sheep out in the hall. Aiding and abetting: all of them accused of a crime they didn't commit.

Mrs. Klas zeroes in on V, closes her rough hand around V's arm. *You two lost a spade last week. I read it in the notes. When you were working in the garden.*

Audra hid the spade, but V keeps that fact a secret, the same way she'll keep secret Audra's shortcut through the corn. Mrs. Klas digs her pointed nails into V's skin, a little path of puckered moons that leave a pale scar. Proof that V didn't snitch.

Where is she? Mrs. Klas spits her hate into V's face.

V hopes Audra's in a truck with some kind stranger. The sharp spade in her hand in case he isn't kind. The only weapon she could take for her protection.

How would I know where she went? V yanks her arm away. *I'm not my brother's keeper.*

You let V go, Big Martha bellows, and the crowd of captive girls falls into chaos.

V's ready for a riot, a mutiny, a strike. She thinks about the Teamsters, how they marched on Minneapolis, how they fought in '34. Mrs. Klas can kill V now; V doesn't care. The weak light through the windows only means more work to come.

*Girls Working in the Field, Minnesota Home School for
Girls at Sauk Centre, ca. 1930*

State School Pastoral

The aproned servants of V's nation swelter in the kitchen canning corn, while the officer, Miss Tate, demands perfection.

Everything V does today is wrong.

The silk threads clinging to the cob. Her shucking slow and sloppy.

Who can't shuck?

A lazy pig like V deserves to starve.

Who does V think she is, the Queen of Sheba?

Miss Tate wants V to crumble, but she won't.

Instead, V shucks the next husk slower still, calls Miss Tate a bitch, hurls her half-shucked cob across the room.

Bitch, V says again into the slap.

The hot welt a badge of courage V is proud to earn.

"This is by no means a cruel institution, but it is true that house mothers sometimes slap their charges, that tubbings have been used as punishment, and that segregation behind bars and isolation on restricted diet are regular punishments."

—Handbook of American Institutions for Delinquent Juveniles,
Vol. 1: West North Central States, 1938

August 12, 1937

Day 469 finds V beneath a willow, a fallen star weeping like the leaves. Shhh, don't tell anyone she cried. The days will never end here. Never end. Just once, she wants to jump that late-night train to Minneapolis, the rumbled lure that calls to her in sleep, whistle, whistle, but V's too small to pull herself into the car. The train's too fast. Caught beneath the wheel, V would be shredded into slaw.

Not the train, but how?

Four-hundred-sixty-nine days for loving Mr. C. For bringing baby June into the world. For entertaining for good money like girls do every day. She's nearly seventeen. Everything in Minneapolis has happened without her. She's a vowel that's been erased. An *I* that doesn't matter to this world.

In the yard the average girls play kickball, lap the bases, while V feigns sick with cramps. Another Sunday afternoon of Recreation. Nest of gnats, the cling of fresh-cut grass against her calves. Next month, for thirty healthful days, V will mow the grounds.

She tries to bolt her heart against the tyranny of numbers. November 3, 1938. Three-hundred-ninety-seven days until she's sent out as a servant.

One-thousand-five-hundred-forty-five, until she's twenty-one and free.

1,545.

She can't last through four long digits; she can't last.

Run

Before milking, in the dark of 5:00 a.m., down the back path past the barrels, through the thin break in the trees, straight into the corn, V and Dodie run. Out of breath, keep running. Knife pain cutting through V's ribs. Ducking in a ditch or waving down a pick-up that won't stop. Neither knows the way to Minneapolis. They piss in waist high weeds, keep running with a rhythm that promises new life. June and June and June inside V's head. The girls that didn't get caught—Audra, Grace, Gazelle—run beside V now. Los Angeles, New York, San Francisco, New Orleans, Chicago, Kansas City, all of these are places they could live. They know the towns from movies; they've seen them on a map. Darting through small backyards lit by moon, or a lamp in someone's window, surviving on small carrots caked with dirt. Wormed green apples off the ground. A swig of whisky, a hunk of bread, offered by a hobo. He's too poor to own a car or he would help. He draws a cross into the dirt, says they're running North when they need South, but Minneapolis isn't safe for two young girls. Murders and the like. All kinds of cunning men riding in on boxcars, jumping off for soup.

Okay, V says, *we'll head someplace else.* A trick in case he snitches to the cops. Run and run.

We can mate for life like doves, dumb Dodie says. *We can raise your girl together. Whatever place you want.* That night, V wakes with Dodie's wet cheek nuzzled in her breast, her hand between V's legs. She won't be Dodie's dove in Minneapolis. But here—

V wonders if her mother has been warned, if she'll prepare a feast like that father in the Bible, or cling to June, report V to the cops. V's mother can't have June. June belongs to V. To keep June is to covet. To steal. V's mother knows the Ten Commandments in English and Norwegian. *Thou shall not.*

Run and run. Rats and mice and bats, abandoned barns, loose dogs, red welts across their legs, mosquito bites and itch weed, snakes, then waiting in a drugstore for a thunderstorm to pass, the county sheriff strolls in calmly with handcuffs for them both.

Girls received during year ending June 30, 1937, by type of admission:

From courts	97
Returned from parole	83
Returned from runaway	20
Transferred	—
Other	23
Total	223

—Statistics for the Minnesota Home School for Girls at Sauk Centre, Minnesota, from Handbook of American Institutions for Delinquent Juveniles, Vol. 1: West North Central States, 1938

Reformation

After the torture of cold tubbings—V forcibly submerged until she's ready to give up—three weeks in isolation, V's curls shaved to the scalp, two weeks of bread and milk, six long grueling months in Pioneer, the prison uniform of blue chambray and bloomers, no general conversation, no recreation, iron bars over her window, V up at 5:00 a.m. to do the laundry for the barn girls, scrub the cow shit from the clothes, filthy shit-soaked water eating at V's skin, birthday without family, Christmas day without a word of June, without a present to her name, every single meal spent in silence, after that, repentant V is broken, and properly reformed.

[Or, perhaps in 1938 punished V was spared the tubbings? I will leave that to the reader to decide.]

"It was the consensus that we emphasized the use of tubbing in a manner disproportionate with its use in the program. Its efficacy was openly questioned and it was reported at that time of the survey that it had not been used for onto two years (and not since). And the attitude was not one of vindictiveness to the offender any more in that treatment than any other."

—*Minnesota Home School for Girls at Sauk Centre refutes the present use of tubbings reported in the* Handbook of American Institutions for Delinquent Juveniles, Vol. 1: West North Central States, 1938

[Why not assume that V was happy,
grateful to be trained,
glad-hearted with the poultry,
content to milk the cows,
adoring of the matron
in a place so like a family home?
Why not believe waking up at 6:00 a.m.
to iron for the officers,
V looked forward to her day?
Looked forward to the laundry:
boiling, hanging, wringer, washboard—
those dark hours in the basement
or being summoned before bed
to wash the hair of the officers?

Why not write that story?
The story of V lucky, saved,
redeemed from her own sins,
rescued by the state?
Why doubt V's compliance at that school?

An inherited distrust of institutions?
My own adolescent refusal to conform?
High school classes spent confined to a dark closet.

Or 1950s June, who despised all things domestic,

who would not cook or clean or sew or iron or care for a sick kid.
June's pathological aversion to homemaking,
a loathing I imagine young V shared.]

February Death

They take Toots out on a stretcher. A public spectacle V watches from the window of her room. Nightgowned girls from Cottage Four sobbing in the snow; the matron trying to shoo them all inside. Dead Toots under a sheet. Suicide, that's the rumor handed from one gossip to the next. Slit wrists. Hung. No one knows for sure.

Toots dead like the tragic showgirl stories V clipped from the *Tribune*. Falling stars leaping out of windows to their deaths. Or the young Minneapolis teacher who jumped from the Franklin Bridge. But where did Toots get the nerve to end it all? To step into the darkness? Did she panic in the end? V needs to know.

Suicide at fourteen.

Tough Toots. V's first friend in Higbee Hospital. The girl who built a shanty underneath the Lake Street bridge. Crooked grin. During that long month in Reception, Toots always had a joke.

V marks a sharp black tally in her heart. She's too young to have a once-friend die, but Toots is dead. After this, other friends will follow. V will die. She hopes it isn't here.

She puffs a patch of fog onto the glass, draws a cross before the stretcher disappears.

Tomorrow someone new will take Toot's seat at supper, someone new will be the third in line. Toots who always snuck a secret wave to V in their two years without speaking.

Hello. Goodbye. Words V didn't get to say. Toots a friend from Higbee Hospital.

A friend.

And now Tough Toots is gone.

[Summer 2016,
I drive out to see the place where V was held—
the cottages where V trained as a domestic,
the land where she once labored,
the hospital where June was born.
Former institution now a home for veterans.
The years of girls all gone,
their stories lost.
Miles of summer corn the girls once canned,
painted buildings white and scabbed,
front pillars peeled away to wood.
The silence of the grass browned by the sun.
That grand administration building
Fannie French Morse ordered on a hill.
A private rise dug out of the school's flat land.
A permanent depression Fannie left after her reign.]

The Third Summer

Bright azaleas in full bloom, V seventeen, and June turns twenty months in Minneapolis. V hopes that in November, for her birthday, her sisters will bring June. She's asked and asked again without an answer. She's promised she won't be locked in Pioneer this time. She needs more than the single tiny photo sent from Rose. She wants to feel June's head of thick black curls, sniff those little ears she used to nibble, see her girl in buckle shoes and gloves. June too far beyond the baby that V held. She needs to cup her daughter's face, lift her to her hip, hear June call her *Mama*.

V records today in pencil on the back of the *McCall's. 6/06/1938. IMYBJ ILY.* Forbidden words V can't write or say, but she has a secret code: first letter of each word she must keep silent. Inside the magazine, the pattern for a dress she'll sew June for her birthday. Sweet sailor dress. Red ribbon trim. V's mother will be proud of her clean seams. The tidy stitches she's perfected at the school.

The dress is all V has to show her steady love for June. Not letters— they won't let V write to June. But years from now, June will have that sailor dress as proof V didn't forget. At eighteen months and twenty, when June turned two and three, every day V held June in her heart.

Or maybe June will never know that V was gone. Will never know these years they spent apart. Lost days erased like dust. No child can remember her first years.

The first thing V remembers is their Grand Avenue apartment. V, probably two or three, marching in a circle while everybody clapped.

Ida, Lydia, and Rose. V's mother, too. V's father's work cap on her head while he sang his favorite song: *Tramp, tramp, tramp, keep on a-tramping. Nothing doing here for you.*

Nothing doing here for V now either. Nothing here, but missing June. *ILYBJ. ILY. ILY. ILY.*

V wonders if her dead father can see June in that basement, if he can watch June like an angel, protect V's dark-haired girl. *Don't let her dance for Ray,* she prays in case her father loves her still.

DDFR, she writes to June. *DDBJ.*

"On leaving the institution almost every girl is placed in a position to give her practical experience in a small home."

—Minnesota Home School for Girls at Sauk Centre,
"Report to Minnesota State Board of Control," June 30, 1936

What V Owns
When She Leaves

1 suitcase

1 coat

1 hat

1 silk dress

1 pair chamoisette gloves

1 nainsook slip

3 pair nainsook bloomers @ 40c

2 cotton crepe nightgowns @ 30c

4 print dresses (2 light) (2 dark) @ 55c

2 cotton vests (if desired) @ 16c

2 pair of cotton hose @ 16c

2 kitchen aprons @ 12c

1 pair going out shoes

1 two-way stretch girdle

1 sanitary belt, 6 outing napkins (and safety pins)

4 handkerchiefs

1 toothbrush

1 tube toothpaste

1 bobby comb

1 small box powder and puff

Also, one pair of good used shoes for work, original cost $2.00

—*Reprinted in the* Handbook of American Institutions for Delinquent Juveniles, Vol. 1: West North Central States, 1938

Release

V packs her suitcase in the matron's room, every school-permitted item carefully inspected, every piece of clothing pressed and clean. The dresses that she made. The handstitched kitchen aprons. Two pair of cotton hose. The few things that she's saved during these years—a pencil sketch she did of June in recreation, Walt Whitman's words she copied down in English ("failing to fetch me at first keep encouraged"), letters from her mother and her sisters, the little gingham bear she'd just begun for June—the matron will discard all that; V doesn't need it now. Parole is not a place for V's mementos. The only thing V is allowed is June's small picture. That, and the last letter sent from Rose. No envelopes with addresses. No papers. No names of girls she knew at school. Those girls should be forgotten. V is starting fresh now on parole. The matron won't say where V is going; V will know when she arrives.

Do your best, the matron warns. *Or you'll be sent back for retraining.*

I will, V vows. As every prisoner vows.

III.

PRACTICAL EXPERIENCE

"Placement of girls on parole continues to be largely in domestic work where they receive the benefit of close association with people who have economic and social security and will take an active personal interest in the girl."

—*Minnesota Home School for Girls at Sauk Centre,*
"Report to the Minnesota State Board of Control," June 30, 1938

"We expect the girl to work faithfully for you. We trust you will remember this girl has not a woman's judgment. Do not expect too much of her. We ask from you a wise, motherly interest in her welfare, so that by your hearty cooperation with the School, the girl may make real development in character in your home. We hope that you will help us to train her to become a good woman and a useful member of society."

—Instructions to Employers, Minnesota Home School for Girls at Sauk Centre. Reprinted in the Handbook of American Institutions for Delinquent Juveniles, Vol. 1: West North Central States, 1938

A Good Woman

Mrs. Taft expected a brunette. Most certainly a house girl larger than a child. She already has a child of her own.

Well, may we, Mrs. Taft? V's visitor asks firmly.

They're stalled outside the Tafts' door in Duluth, V's goose-pimpled girl legs burning from the cold. The great gusts from Lake Superior blowing the hat off of her head.

Is that an ill wind? Mrs. Taft sniffs, and V sees the misgiving in those eyes. Mrs. Taft has changed her mind about a girl the likes of V. She doesn't want V's trouble in her house.

Really, Mrs. Taft, V's visitor insists. V's "visitor" not a friendly visitor, but a field agent for parole. *We'll catch our death of cold out in this night.*

Mrs. Taft opens the carved oak door just enough to let them pass. Her dear son upstairs with a slight fever; these two must mind their noise. *The girl may set her bag down on the floor.*

V unloads the school-issued suitcase, takes in her towering new mistress in the belted rayon dress. Puffed sleeved. Padded shoulders. A shirred bodice that her mother would admire. A polished egg-white face. Thin gold hair crimped into perfect waves.

I wouldn't imagine you've been in a house like this, she says to V.

V's stood in grander mansions while her mother measured drapes, measured breasts and hips and waists, the shoulders of small girls. Still there's enough work to be done in this large house—three meals a day to make, miles of oak to polish, ten windows in this sitting room alone, a fireplace to sweep, expensive rugs to beat, a little boy to tend—V isn't going to wish she had more work.

No ma'am, V lies, demurely. *It's truly marvelous. Magnificent.* V knows Mrs. Taft expects demure. Mrs. Taft won't be the school's fabled mistress who treats V like a daughter. V knows that from the failures on parole—girls returned or run away, all sent back to Sauk Centre for readjustment or retraining—you ask those girls, they'll say their parole homes were all cruel. A loving family a lie the school tells.

Well, Mrs. Taft says, nodding toward the street. *The girl is in good hands now. I shall see to her myself.*

But Mrs. Taft—this is not a visitor easily dismissed. She has her practiced lecture to deliver; V's endured it twice already on the drive from Sauk Centre to Duluth. But V will listen for a third time in order to impress. The litany of improvements for V to cultivate: propriety, chastity, and hygiene. The skills to run a proper home. *I'm afraid we still have more details to discuss,* V's visitor insists. Placement rules to be reviewed: No contact with strangers in Duluth. Constant supervision. The darkness in V's future if she fails at this chance.

Received and read last week, Mrs. Taft says, before the visitor can speak. *For now, you are dismissed. If I'm in need of more direction—*

But Madame, if I may—

You may not, Mrs. Taft says briskly. *Rest assured, dear woman, I know how to train a girl.*

Housewarming

1.

New room, new hope, new morning. A small twin bed against a papered wall. A three-drawer bureau of her own. A round mirror V won't share with other girls.

The other girls all gone.

The girls?

Milking cows and boiling porridge, wringing laundry without V. Shouldn't V be relieved to leave those other girls? To live outside that institution? Shouldn't she be ecstatic to finally have a home?

2.

It's Mrs. Taft who yanks V's curtains open, tells V not to linger when work needs to be done. It's already past 6:30; V's expected to be dressed. Didn't V keep a schedule at the school? Frankie's awake and hungry; Sunday biscuits must be baked. The doctor likes his breakfast before church.

He'll be in the parlor with his paper and his pipe. Please put yourself together so the doctor's not alarmed. We have standards in this family you must follow.

3.

Downstairs, V finds freckled Frankie amused with two small trains and Dr. Taft setting aside his pipe and Sunday paper to offer V his clammy hand. (His apologies, he was needed at the hospital last night when V arrived.) Not exactly Cary Grant, but distinguished in the way tall rich men are. Satin smoking jacket. Long legs crossed at the knee. He takes a slow draw from his pipe, studies V's small body the way a doctor would. *So, I understand you danced,* he says with a slight smile. *A showgirl in your day?* He gives a little laugh like V's job was a joke.

Sang, V says. She knows exactly what he's asking. Nearly three years kept from men, but V remembers well. *I sing.*

Still? he says, surprised. *You haven't given up that calling?*

Sing! Frankie shouts. *You sing a song for me!*

Maybe later, Dr. Taft winks. *I doubt V's songs are meant for a young boy.*

[The fallacy of erasure.
The fallacy of a clean slate, of starting fresh.
The fallacy of new beginnings,
of self-invention,
of good girl, bad girl.
The fallacy of being born a child
like any other child.
The fallacy of bootstraps.
The fallacy of self-improvement.
The fallacy of education. Of amnesia.
The fallacy of training and retraining.
The fallacy of effort,
of merit and de-merit.
The fallacy of servants *just like family*.
The fallacy of family.
The fallacy of earning or deserving.
The fallacy of opportunity,
of chances granted by sweet charity.
The fallacy of handouts,
gifts, as if you haven't paid.
The fallacy of reclamation
and reform.]

Motherly Interest

V's first Saturday in service, Mrs. Taft dons a seal fur for an afternoon of shopping in Duluth. A trip out of the house V might enjoy.

Downtown Duluth, no bigger than a sliver of the city V once loved, the streets where she once sang. Yet, after years trapped in the country, every street noise rattles her raw nerves. V startles at the honking. The rush of people walking past.

If anyone should ask, you're just an ordinary house girl. Not a word about that school, you understand? Or God forbid, parole. I wouldn't want anyone to think—

Of course, V says, eager to be finished with her last role as a delinquent. A slate wiped clean like Rose after divorce. Also, Mrs. Taft likes V to say, *Of course.*

Down Superior, past the jeweler and the drugstore, the butcher and the baker, beneath the street car wires, V trails Mrs. Taft from shop to shop. Schlepping, as Mr. C would say. V's arms aching from the weight of bags and boxes Mrs. Taft has filled.

It's good to have a new girl. Do your best.

Of course, V says again, well-versed in how a new girl must behave. A new girl must compliment Mrs. Taft's ivory slip selection, the three expensive winter dresses, the topaz pendant so lovely on her skin, the adorable fur-collar coat she bought for Frankie. V bears another package, sniffs the Shalimar when ordered, agrees the hint of citrus is all wrong, admires the grand piano Mrs. Taft expects for Christmas.

V a stand-out star in her first Duluth performance, until Mrs. Taft spies the marquee for a double-feature at the theater in town. GIRLS' SCHOOL and REFORMATORY.

How perfectly disgusting, Mrs. Taft says. *Who would make a movie of your life?*

Home Making and
Home Management

Each morning after breakfast, V must mop the kitchen floor while Mrs. Taft inspects, concerned. *A home is not an institution; a family kitchen must be kept clean at all times.* There—a film of scummy lather or a place V left a streak, a rim of suds against the wooden rail.

V must learn to get it right if she wants a good report. *Training tells,* Mrs. Taft warns V. Three years of good work here, and V can be a housemaid for a family in St. Paul. Or was it Minneapolis where V lived? At any rate, a girl who keeps a clean house will find work.

Or I could bring my daughter to Duluth, V says. *I could take care of your family and June, too. Couldn't we ask the school to send her? The visitor?*

I'm not one to fan false hopes, Mrs. Taft says quickly, then she's off to Ladies' Aid, leaving V with bratty Frankie and a wooden chest of tarnished silver to be cleaned. V could steal a spoon or poke a fork in Frankie's eye. Frankie with his shrill, incessant whine: *I want, I want.*

I want, too, V snaps at Frankie. *I want to bust your chops, kid. Bust loose from this place. Get home to my own girl.*

Stop it, Frankie scolds. *You're supposed to play with me.*

Home again from meeting, Mrs. Taft must reinstruct on how to keep a toilet clean. Rotate daily scrubbings of vinegar and bleach. *You know men can leave a mess, even little men like Frankie.*

And learn what to discuss, Mrs. Taft continues, while V on hands and knees must scour grout and marble for whatever errant pee she might have missed. *Frivolous affairs,* Mrs. Taft advises. *Or flowers. A girl may always speak of flowers.*

School Days, Night Life Mix

I'd like to see you in that, V, Dr. Taft says, handing V his precious daily paper. The doctor always friendly when Mrs. Taft has left the room. Full of jokes and winks that V can't trust. *You have that dress packed in your suitcase? By all means replace that frowsy apron with a costume like this girl's.*

V looks down at the newspaper, the first one she's been allowed to read in years, and there on the front page, under the headline "School Days, Night Life Mix," dual photos of a schoolgirl and showgirl. Frances Smith, 18, of Brooklyn living V's two lives. Left-side schoolgirl Frances plain-faced, sweet naïve, clean white blouse and dull black shoes, studious, posing for the camera with her papers and books. Right-side showgirl Frances primping in a mirror, preparing for the stage, a sultry showgirl pressing powder to her chin. Beautiful bare arms, one milky shoulder draped by sheer chiffon, shapely legs men will applaud, a flimsy slip of dress meant to be discarded.

I'd like to see you in that, V, Dr. Taft repeats. *See one of your numbers.*

V stares at New York's Frances Smith in her bracelets and her bow, her strappy gold high heels, bright and shimmering like the ones V used to wear. Frances working nights to support her widowed mother. Frances Smith the front-page showgirl V once longed to be. A heroine. A star. A girl worthy of a headline.

A New York showgirl free to lead V's double-life while V labors for the Tafts.

For What We Are about
to Receive

Thankful. Grateful. Blessed. Beholden and obliged. V reaping the daily benefits of close association with good people. Doesn't V feel gratitude today and every day?

A house girl at the table. It's unheard of, one guest says.

After V presents the turkey, she may take the seat near Frankie. V shouldn't draw attention to herself.

It's all that Christian charity, Dr. Taft says with a wink. *And Martha's mother was a suffragette, you know.*

Well still, another guest tells Dr. Taft. *Your family is too kind.*

V slices Frankie's dark meat, forks away the skin, spoons a divot in his stuffing so the gravy will stay pooled. Promises the wishbone if he's good.

That's not for you to say, V, Mrs. Taft corrects. *Mind your place.*

Of course, V says, her eyes lowered toward her plate, the polished silver fork heavy in her hand.

I might like one of my own girls, a woman says. Mrs. Day or Ray or May, V can't remember. Too many pearl-necked women at this table to keep track. *I could use a girl to watch little Paul, he wears me out.*

Me, too, another says. *I'd like a live-in girl.*

Well, it isn't without labor, Mrs. Taft says with a deep sigh. V was up at 4:00 a.m. to dress the turkey, bake the rolls. *It takes the patience of a saint to train a girl.*

I'm sure. Paul's mother nods.

Outside, Duluth November is a desert of white wind, a vast expanse of arctic between V and the world. V dreams a silver bridge of ice to Minneapolis, dreams her family at the table, the railroad worker dead. A scene from *Little Women. At last,* her sisters cheer, *our little Amy's home.*

V dabs a taste of stuffing to June's lips. Cranberries. Creamed corn. June makes a little face and they all laugh.

Let Frankie feed himself, Mrs. Taft scolds V.

Of course, V mumbles, waking from the dream of June to Frankie's constant scowl.

V could drown from lonely.

V could drown.

Fa La La La La La La La La

1.

In the downstairs of Wahl's Department Store, homesick V feels the tug of Toyland. The promise of bright packages and bows, the smell of pine, the colored bulbs, the tinsel, all she wants for June, and all that she can't give to her this Christmas. June standing in the line to visit Santa. June lifted to the reindeer, posing for a picture in a little velvet coat.

2.

The Toyland reindeer's fake, so Frankie throws a tantrum, kicks its life-less flanks the way he would a horse. *Look,* he screams, *the eyes are made of marbles. Santa's reindeer's dead.*

Oh sweetheart, Mrs. Taft says.

Frankie's inconsolable, and still he wants and wants. Trucks and trains and cars, a cowboy suit, the fancy one with fur, a lariat, a gun, all the candy he can eat, two teddy bears, a tent, a tub of chocolate ice cream, pudding in his bed, two candy canes, today, no, four or five. *That ought to do it, son,* Santa says, pushing Frankie off to V.

Santa doesn't even ask if he's been good.

A perfect painted tea set, porcelain and rose. V lifts a tiny cup, imagines June opening the gift on Christmas morning. Imagines June playing party with a tea set. Pretty Christmas gift from Mommy. Mommy loves her girl.

$1.60. V hasn't saved that yet, but Mrs. Taft could give her credit.

I don't think so, Mrs. Taft says, taking the teacup from V's fingers. *No payment in advance. Didn't you read the rules? And even then, only money for necessities. Credit is a weakness common to the poor.*

4

Mrs. Taft offers V a gift choice from their charity donations: Old toys scavenged from the shelves in Frankie's closet—a wooden top, dull puzzles, a book of Mother Goose, a set of baby blocks. *There should be something here that suits June,* Mrs. Taft assures. *And I won't deduct the postage from your pay.*

V finds a small stuffed bear in the bottom of the box, scrubs the jam stain from its fur, makes sure it smells likes soap before she wraps it in a box.

That's mine, Frankie sobs, and so it is.

Christmas Morning 1938

In celebration of Christ's birth, V prepares the Christmas breakfast of spiced peaches warmed with cream, soft caramel rolls, coffee, the Christmas sausage V bought from the butcher.

For Mrs. Taft, a diamond watch from the good doctor. A set of diamond earrings. No Christmas morning grand piano though, and so she pouts.

Scotch again for me, the doctor jokes. *And another set of cufflinks! An opera record ordered from New York!*

Toys and trucks and cars and trains and color crayons for Frankie, but best of all that cowboy suit from Wahl's: red suedine vest and pants, fur-lined down the front, silver ornaments that jangle when he walks. *The sheriff's come to town,* he says with a mean swagger. A lariat and hat. Neckerchief. Gun and holster at his hip.

(And what did V send June? That wrinkled Mother Goose book with Frankie's name on the first page. The Jack Sprat rhyme torn down the middle. All June will have this morning to know her mother's love.)

Bang bang, Frankie shouts, and V must fall down to the floor or Frankie cries. *You're dead,* he says, *so die.*

And how merry for you, V, the doctor says. *To spend your holiday inside a family home.*

Of course, V says. V must always say *of course.*

"If you find the girl disobedient, do not wait until the regular call from the visitor, but let her know at once. You should not transfer the girl to any other place or let her visit friends or have friends visit her without permission of the School or its agent.

If for any cause you desire to have the girl removed, consult your parole visitor.

THE GIRL MUST NOT BE LEFT ALONE ALL NIGHT with the woman of the house away unless there is a responsible woman in charge."

—*Instructions to Employers, Minnesota Home School for Girls at Sauk Centre, 1937. Reprinted in the* Handbook of American Institutions for Delinquent Juveniles, Vol. 1: West North Central States, 1938

Personal Interest

From the door of his dark den, Dr. Taft insists V enjoy an opera. V begs to be excused, but he won't have it. *You've seen plays I would presume?*

At school, of course, V says, taking her place on the edge of his settee, her legs locked at the ankles, her hands locked in her lap. V could say she's been a star—the Little Match Girl in sixth grade, the lead in the eighth-grade operetta—but she doesn't want to be a girl that Dr. Taft knows well.

Doctor, jeweler, judge: V understands what men want with a girl.

Mrs. Taft at bridge and tea? Who else is in this house?

Frankie napping in the nursery. Only Frankie.

V could scream into the silence; she's tempted to scream now.

But here is Dr. Taft, setting the needle down on *Manon*, closing the door to his dark study. Dr. Taft insisting V acquire culture and this is where it starts.

"When we divide the people of a given society into a pyramidic structure of upper, middle, and lower classes it soon becomes evident that the greatest number of social problems invariably occur near the base of the configuration. This is due to the nature and composition of society and the individuals who populate each stratum. Just why delinquency always appears there seems inexplicable. The important fact for the scholar is that maladjustment is more serious at the bottom of the pyramid."

—*Walter A. Lunden,* Juvenile Delinquency:
Manual and Source Book, *1936*

Dr. Taft Imagines France

At the bottom of the pyramid, V vacates her ravished body while Dr. Taft imagines France. *Parlez vous Français? Oui Oui. Bonjour. Bonne nuit. Say Merci, Mademoiselle. Embrassez moi. Embrassez.*

Moulin Rouge. You dance at the Moulin Rouge?

French, the secret language V must learn while Mrs. Taft's asleep, or bathing in the morning, or tucking darling Frankie into bed.

Encore! Oh Oui!

V made to bend over the washtub or forced down to her knees. *Je t'aime, ma belle.* His maladjusted showgirl and his house girl, gagging down the taste of Dr. Taft.

[The inheritance of silence.
Silence as survival.]

The First Time V Considers

The house eerily empty, V sitting at *His* desk admiring *Her* drapes, settles on those silver braided cords. Wouldn't one make a perfect noose around V's neck?

The plaster lion watches. The lion has been kind, he will not judge. Quiet as he's been, he's talking now to V.

Why not just go to death? the lion asks. *What is on this side to keep you here?*

V feels the darkness calling like it did inside the Uptown, the beautiful black moment before the movie would begin.

This could be the last scene in the movie of V's life. The ravished house girl seemingly asleep beside a statue. A silken silver cord around her neck. A note beside her body telling Mrs. Taft the truth.

Why not? the lion whispers. *So many stars have quit.*

V a small domestic tragedy, until she rises like the phoenix finished with this world.

Mrs. Taft's Assessment

Before she posts it to the State, Mrs. Taft finds it only right to share her January assessment. If V wishes to improve, she should know her failings and her faults. Of course, Mrs. Taft would like to praise, because some days, albeit too few, she wishes to believe that V does try.

Yes, V has several tasks she can do well: soft boiling breakfast eggs, preparing roasted chicken—V's beef roasts are always over-cooked—oiling the mahogany, brushing the lint from Dr. Taft's suits, keeping the upstairs hallway swept, but V won't win a medal for her meals or her room. Her drawers look like a hurricane has hit. Private garments willy-nilly. And she often lets her socks sag at the ankle.

V's ironing remains a constant failure; unsightly creases have been found on tablecloths and clothes, and Dr. Taft too often needs his shirts re-pressed. More than once he's had to venture to the basement to reprimand the girl.

Mrs. Taft can't say that V complains, and yet the girl exudes a chronic insolence when tending to her chores, or entertaining Frankie, or tidying his toys. As if she isn't grateful for all the Tafts have done. But perhaps most disconcerting, is her senseless, ceaseless longing for that daughter. How can V attend their child when she's preoccupied with hers?

In short, while home training will continue, they are sorely unimpressed.

Still, despite V's many flaws, they wish her well.

"The function of parole is not just protection from temptation but directing the girl not to succumb to temptation."

—*Minnesota Home School for Girls at Sauk Centre,*
"Report to Minnesota State Board of Control," June 30, 1936

Ladies' Aid

Jimmy Washington is all V has for hope. Pimpled, buck-toothed Jimmy working at the butcher, wrapping V's order of cut beef in clean, white paper, or smoking on the sidewalk when he knows V will arrive. Monday mornings before the butcher even opens, V is always there to buy fresh chops. The doctor only eats his pork chops fresh.

Swell coat, Jimmy calls this morning, as V walks up the street. *Cute curls. Hey there, toots.* A whistle now for V. *I sure do like those eyes.*

V's only friend in this cold city, and he's more opportunity than friend. *I'm in a jam,* V frets to Jimmy. *I'm dying for the word from Minneapolis, but you know that I can't get it at the Tafts. If my brother sends a letter, those skunks will read it first.*

The Tafts. He rolls his eyes. Before V did the shopping, Jimmy had to cut the meat for Mrs. Taft. *That broad was never happy.* He's told V that before. *Heck, you want to use my address, V? Tell your brother to send his letters to my rooming house on Bank Street. 601 West Bank Street. Soon as one arrives, I'll deliver it myself.*

Jimmy puffs a cloud of Camel smoke into the bitter wind, readjusts the sidewalk sign to make a show of work.

You got a Camel for me, Jimmy? V hasn't smoked a cigarette since that terrible day at Lu's, but Jimmy's offer of an address makes V's young heart run wild. She's going to ditch this place. Write to Mr. C, get out of town. Mr. C will save her. *You're my knight in shining armor. You keep my brother's letter for me, I'll get it from you here.*

Sure thing, doll, Jimmy says, giving V that friendly wink. (Even home-ly boys are winking in the story of V's life.) *You give old Jimmy's address to your brother. Old Jimmy's here to help.*

". . . Only now and then, one born under a lucky star is adopted and educated by large-minded foster parents who recognize that the illegitimate is not responsible for having come into this world under conditions opposed to the best interest of society."

—*Maurice A. Bigelow*, Sex-Education: A Series of Lectures Concerning Knowledge of Sex in Its Relation to Human Life, *1916*

A Lucky Star

On a day that's winter blue, in a Nash Hank bought on credit (V rushes to the window hoping for the Ford), Rose and Hank suddenly arrive. Hank holding Rose's hand like she's a girl. Hank broad-faced and early-bald, less handsome than the fleeting husband Rose divorced.

I bet that you're surprised, Rose says. (Stunned would be a better word.) Rose and Hank acting like two lovebirds in the parlor at the Tafts? Taking a sudden Sunday drive up to Duluth?

And now inexplicably V's visitor is here, stamping snow loose from her boots, shaking hands with Rose and Hank and Mrs. Taft. Handing an orange candy stick to Frankie. The visitor V hasn't seen in months.

V feels a wheel turn toward some new darkness. An unexpected gathering, like the day Rose walked across the playground to tell V their father died. Rose a stranger at V's recess; Rose a stranger here.

June? V asks, seized by mother-terror that nearly stills her voice.

A handful, Rose says, glowing, *but so sharp. Talk talk talk. Another time we'll bring her. You won't believe how much she's grown.*

I'd really like that, Rose, V says. V knows her daughter's growing; she's imagined every inch. *I would. You can drive up any day. And Mother?* Is that why Rose is here?

Still not fond of cars, Hank says, but that isn't what V asked.

Well anyway, Rose rattles like an ordinary day. *Surprise! Hank and I got married! Married!* So now Rose and V may kiss. *A small service after Christmas! Nothing fancy.*

How wonderful! the visitor agrees, a stack of tidy papers in her lap. *And how wonderful for you, V.*

Wonderful for V? Have Rose and Hank come to take V home? Is that the Sunday secret no one's said? *Do you two already have a place?* V asks, excited. Maybe V and June will live with Rose.

Yes, Rose says. *On Elliot off Lake. Not far from Sears. We're at Thirty-Fourth. A homey second floor apartment.* (Hank rub-rubbing Rose's hand, tap-tapping his left foot like he's impatient.) *Well-heated. And June is with us, too.*

June? She's not with Mother anymore? Does she have a little room? A little room that V and June could share?

She does, Hank says. (V doesn't want to hear from Hank.) *Rose fixed it up real nice.*

So, you don't mind, then? Rose asks sweetly, her gloves still in her hands, a second question hidden in the first.

V looks from Rose to Hank to Mrs. Taft. To the visitor with papers. What is it in this news that V should mind? June out of the railroad worker's reach?

Mind what? V asks.

If Hank. If Hank and I—

They've petitioned for adoption, Mrs. Taft announces. *In the best interest of the child.*

I have the paperwork in order, the visitor chimes in. *The home study was conducted. She's a lucky little girl.*

No, V says. *No adoption. June is mine. You can't have her, Rose.* Now Dr. Taft watches from the doorway of his den. V outnumbered five to one, and still she fights. *Why can't I raise her here? Find a room where we could live? She won't be any bother while I work.*

You're hardly fit to be a mother, Mrs. Taft says sternly. *And that child isn't yours, V.*

She is, V says, forced to hide her temper so she doesn't lose parole. *I'm the one who had her.*

But Hank already loves her like his own. Rose's anxious face moving between love and regret. *He's so good with her, he is. I promise she'll have everything—*

And what would I be then, June's aunt? No, V says again. She's eighteen; they can't make her sign. *I'm her mother, Rose. Why can't I just go home and raise her now? Live with you and Hank? All of us together? We can be a family. I'm not the girl I was, I swear—*

That isn't going to work, Hank says. *We want her to be ours.*

Quite naturally, Mrs. Taft agrees. *And doesn't V have three more years to serve?*

One-thousand-twenty-seven days to be exact.

Letter

Letter up V's sleeve. Literally. Letter tucked between V's arm and winter coat. Letter on Dr. Taft's Italian paper, stolen from the left drawer of his desk. Last chance letter asking Mr. C to save her. Save June. Letter that can't say exactly all that V endures, but Mr. C can read between the lines. *You remember what those men tried at the Cascade?* He still has a promise left to keep. *Things are critical. Acute.* Two desperate words V's learned from Dr. Taft.

But first the inquisition from the mistress: *Where will you walk, V? When will you return?* Thursdays 1:00 to 3:00 are V's free hours, the only time that she's entitled, and still she must account for every step.

The public library, of course, V says, stepping out the doorway. If the letter is discovered, she'll be sent back to Sauk Centre, locked in isolation, tubbed, and shaved, and starved. But worse, the clock begins again.

Now V is outside breathing, breathing snow, and lake, and cloud, the distant drone of train giving her hope. Last chance letter to be sent. *Hello from Little Fox. Remember me?* Letter asking for a ticket, or Mr. C can drive up to Duluth. Bring June. They can cross the border into Canada. If he sends a time and date to V's friend Jimmy, she'll be ready to escape. *Rose wants to steal our daughter, wants to keep her. Do you ever go to see her, Cousin Harold?*

Letter asking if there's love. Or was there ever love? Secret letter. Mr. C can't tell a living soul. Letter saying he lived free. He did. All this time, a man about his business. A man in Minneapolis.

Letter saying not to worry: If he doesn't want to marry V, she'll raise June on her own.

What V Hears from Mr. C

Depleted

Was V smoking with that boy outside the butcher, the doctor wants to know? Again? Hasn't he forbidden V already? Hasn't she been punished? (He has; she has. V no longer cares.) *I had to hear it from a patient,* the doctor says. *Again.*

V's been bad again, Frankie says, hungry for V's blood. *You forbid her, Father. Better punish V.*

Mrs. Taft with her red lips bent in a frown. Pinching her pearl earrings, the way she does when she's upset. *I don't know how much longer I can do this,* she laments to Dr. Taft, as if V's not at their oven forking porkchops on a plate.

You want to be a common whore, V? Dr. Taft asks. *Smoking on the street? Haven't you learned anything?* Dr. Taft just like her mother's husband without the menthol salve and limp.

It doesn't seem so, Mrs. Taft says. *I'm honestly depleted. And I won't have that kind of girl—*

What's a whore? Frankie wants to know. V sets the porkchops on the table, turns to get the green beans sweet with bacon. She'd spit into their beans if they weren't watching her right now.

Please let us eat in peace, Mrs. Taft says with a sigh. *Go up to your room, V.*

I'll work with her, the doctor says.

No, Mrs. Taft says, snatching the crystal bowl of beans out of V's hand. *What more can we do to help this girl?*

"Parolees may be returned at the discretion of the parole agents for violation of parole or for readjustment and retraining. If returned for violation of parole they lose their parole status and must be reparoled by the Board of Control."

—Handbook of American Institutions for Delinquent Juveniles,
Vol. 1: West North Central States, 1938

PAROLED CHILDREN

Returned to Institution:

Temporarily	5
Illness	17
Homes unsuitable	1
Employment unsuitable	1
Misconduct	45
Other causes	40
Died on Parole	2

—Minnesota Home School for Girls at Sauk Centre,
"Report of Population for Month Ending November 30, 1935"

Hide and Seek

Frankie in the playroom with his guns. Mrs. Taft in town to have her waves refreshed. The selfless doctor gone to work.

V hunts the hidden places for their cash. Cash or coins, she'll keep either one. Papers beneath the mattress, tins, bedside books, the row of empty handbags on the shelf. Dr. Taft's wool suits. Every crack and crevice V can find.

Room by room, methodical, silent as the snow.

How much will it cost to rent a room for her and June? In Madison, Milwaukee, Chicago, or Detroit.

How much will it cost to catch a train to Mr. C? Mr. C will have the money to get V out of town.

V can't serve another day of her parole. Can't endure the doctor. He should pay for what he takes, he owes that much to V. She can't let June be raised without her mother, she just can't. She needs to get her daughter.

V! Frankie screams. *You need to play with me now!*

V slips the garnet Christmas cufflink in her bra. Maybe she can pawn it in Duluth. Or sell one garnet cufflink to a stranger on the street, the way V and Em used to sell V's songs.

But what good is one cufflink?

V! he screams again. *You promised hide and seek!*

She did.

A set of two is what V needs. A pair. A pair might buy a ticket. Two.

V and June a pair. Now V tucks the second cufflink in her sock. Mother-daughter cufflinks. Mother-daughter hide and seek. Mother-daughter running from parole.

Wicked

At last V is the wicked girl, unraveled. Locking Frankie in the basement in a game of hide and seek. Nothing but a coat to keep her warm. A pair of stolen cuff links. June's picture in the pocket of her coat. V can't be bothered packing, can't haul a suitcase on the run. Can't listen to those basement screams, Frankie's frantic pounding at the door. Or risk Mrs. Taft home early. Mrs. Taft who wants V to be gone. Gone is where she'll be. So far gone they'll never find her. No one ever will. V gone from their front door. Running past the wide-eyed witness beating a rug clean in the wind. *What's the hurry, little missy, house on fire?* V running down the street. Running between houses. Running toward the tracks. The train. Toward the highway out of town. V that wicked running house girl the good Tafts tried to help.

[Put her on the train,
the bus,
on the floor of a back seat,
or waving down a ride on 61—
a beautiful small girl
shivering in snow.
Child-girl.

Who doesn't want to help
a pretty girl?

Put her at the pawnshop
with her cufflinks for fresh cash.

The only proof of V's escape
discovered in the school's daily ledger of minutia:

V escaped parole.]

"We would also recommend that the present rigid routine of punishment for returned parole violators be modified. Success or failure on parole depends upon so many factors over and above the girl's willingness to succeed that it seems hardly fair to subject every violator to the rigorous punishment of ten days in isolation and several weeks or months in segregation."

—Handbook of American Institutions for Delinquent Juveniles,
Vol. 1: West North Central States, 1938

[And because V's not only V,
but in the company of thousands,
I examine other pages
from the school's daily ledger.
One January week:
Betty J escaped parole.
Ruby L escaped parole.
Marian H escaped parole.
Lorraine D escaped parole.
Four girls in seven days.

And from another in November:
Gwendolyn R was returned.
Gladys O was returned.
Candace T was returned.
Three girls in six days failed at parole.

I will leave you to the white space of parole.]

Minneapolis

The city stalled by snow just as V remembers; V trudging through the alley in her dull gray winter coat. Weighty dense flakes clinging to her curls. Her stiff hands in her pockets, her wool mittens at the Tafts. Cold men huddle in the cracks between garages, children too. Lucky V, the new escapee indecipherable in snow. Now, V walking east on Lake Street, the parking lot of Sears nearly empty. To the north the city skyline paper-white. The whole city disappearing, and yet V knows exactly where she is, knows the streets of Minneapolis like her skin. A city snowstorm like that blizzard she shared with Mr. C, the two of them sleeping or not sleeping, curled together on their coats until the morning route was cleared. Mr. C carrying high-heeled V out to his Ford to deliver her to Em's in time for junior high. Mr. C, her second stop tonight in Minneapolis. June first: June always first. Then, Little Fox and her sweet daughter will step into the warm Cascade Club like two small snowy ghosts.

Homecoming

1.

In an alley east of Elliot, hands and feet frozen stiff and numb, V lurks behind a dumpster in the dark, watches as Rose walks across a room of golden light, bends down at the waist, stands, then bends again. In that second-floor apartment, June is playing on the floor. Surely when Rose bends, she bends to June.

V needs to get to June before Hank comes home from the brake shop. Growing up, Rose couldn't say no to V. In their roles from *Little Women*, Rose played the patient Beth to V's Amy. V the spoiled youngest sister Rose tried to indulge. Benevolent Rose will want V to be happy; she's always wanted that. Of course, she's fond of June, but Rose and Hank will have a baby of their own.

Present, past, and future, June belongs to V. A baby needs her mother; Rose will understand.

V has to take June now before the cops come on their hunt. The law will look. The law will capture V and lock her at Sauk Centre.

Rose walks to the window, glances at the alley, then draws the drapes against the snow.

No, Rose says when V is at her door. *I can't let you in; you know I can't. They're looking for you, V.*

Please, V pleads, showing her white fingers. *I'm freezing. I just need to get warm. I've been running since this morning.*

And why? Rose says, disgusted. *Now you'll start at the beginning. You'll be sent back to that school, and who knows after that? Prison for your life? Is that what you want, V?*

No, V says. *Please don't be angry with me, Rose.*

You've squandered every chance you've ever had. We spoiled you, we did.

Rose, V begs. *At least let me get warm.*

I can't, Rose says again. *I don't want trouble with police. They've already been to Mother's. You can't know the worry that you are. How fragile Mother is now. How much you've put her through. And now to be so selfish with those papers. To deny our poor sweet Margaret—*

Margaret? V says, afraid that she might vomit at that word. *You can't call June "Margaret." She's not your daughter, Rose.*

She is, Rose says. *Who has been her mother, V? These past two years? Who has?*

3.

June playing on a rag rug. June laying her fancy doll down in the cradle, little wooden rocker Hank made for her last Christmas. A head of wild black curls. Mr. C's dark eyes. *You know me. June?* V asks, slipping into the apartment.

June? V tries again, but June won't look in V's direction.

It's Margaret, Rose says sternly. *She only goes by Margaret.*

4.

Not Margaret. Not ever.

Come here, come here, sweet baby. I want to see you, honey girl. V wants June to run into her arms, but June's indifferent. She's too busy with her doll, holding her upside down by one black shoe, rocking that homemade cradle back and forth. Singing rock-a-bye the way V did in nursery. Do you remember how we waltzed? V wants to ask, but their waltzes won't mean anything to June.

5.

And how could you? Rose starts in. *After the school worked so hard to find you that fine home.*

Not so fine, V says. *It wasn't fine.*

Well, fine enough, Rose argues. *You're eighteen, V. When will you grow up?*

6.

June with her nonsense child chatter talk talk talk, still won't look at V. *Do you know who I am?* V asks kneeling on the rug beside her daughter,

Don't you dare ask that, Rose fumes. *Don't do that to our girl.*

7.

V calculates the distance between June and the door, how quickly she could grab her, how quickly they could run. V and June slipping down the streets of Minneapolis, slipping toward the Cascade Club or where?

8.

You see Em still? V asks. Em will hide them in her attic. Loyal Em will help. *Gone, too,* Rose says, relieved. *California last I heard.*

9.

Three long years of dreams and this is home.

10.

Don't go to Mother's place. Ray hates you, V.

11.

What's this? Hank growls, home from work too early, a cap of snow covering his head. June racing toward the door to knot her arms around his leg. *What in God's name is your sister doing here? Shouldn't she be with that doctor in Duluth?*

Hank looks around confused. Wet V. No suitcase at the door.

She's run away, Rose sighs.

Then she should run, Hanks says. Cigarettes and grease V can smell across the room. Hank in filthy station grays. Industrious or not, V wants more for June than Hank will earn. Bully Hank. *We can't hide her here,* he says, scooping June into his arms. *How's Daddy's little girl, how is my Margaret?*

Honey, Rose begs sweetly. *I can't send my sister out into this snow.*

12.

Hank can. Hank can drive down to the drugstore, call up the police. Or he'll knock now at the neighbor's; the neighbors have a phone. Hank holding June too close in his thick arms.

Daddy mad, June says, and Hank nods yes.

I want you gone, he says to V. *On your own or with the police. We don't need you here.*

Can't you drive her, Hank? Rose pleads. *Can't you take her to the Cascade Club at least. Let Mr. C do what he can to help her; I know he truly cares.*

First, she signs the papers. She signs, I'll take her there.

Attachment Theory: Two

June, held safe in Rose's arms, watches from the window as that strange girl leaves with Hank. Black dot in thick snow. Girl who didn't belong in their apartment. Bad girl June wants to be gone.

Bye-bye, June waves out to the night, and Rose waves, too.

Yes, Rose says, *bye-bye.*

June, the lucky little foundling, the precious only child secure now in a future she can't see through the snow. Private schools and parties, a new dress for every dance, cashmere and pearls, college at sixteen. A small house from Rose and Hank for her first marriage. A second marriage, a second little house. Rose and Hank nearby to raise her children. Lucky June, watching this moment from the window, always wants the moon and stars and so they're hers.

I want a candy, she tells Rose, turning from the trouble, turning from that strange girl who left in Daddy's car.

Oh you! Rose laughs, kissing June's small nose.

And even though it's time for supper, and June's favorite hot dish is ready in the oven—cheese potatoes with little bits of ham—Rose carries June into the kitchen, lifts the glass lid to the sweet jar, and lets June make her choice.

[EVIDENCE OF V: AUGUST 1975, MINNEAPOLIS

I track June to her bedroom, cool cave of basement darkness where she escapes her teenaged kids. Rumpled bed, make-up stains on dingy pillows, a drugstore bottle of Ciara the single decoration on her dresser. Disheveled open drawers I've often searched for some dark secret. The reason that June disappears for boats, and friends, and parties. June and her doting second husband leaving us for days without a word.

Hey, I say, watching her reflection in the mirror. June a beauty still, her lipsticked mouth open in an *O* as she brushes on mascara. June will put on make-up and be gone. *I've been thinking about something.*

What else is new? June says with a laugh. *You're always thinking.* It's true, I am, but my quick brain is the one trait June admires.

I've been thinking, I say again to June's reflection. My reflection. Green-eyed to June's brown eyes. Faded jersey. Wild, frizzy hair. June's nervous middle daughter prone to irrational suspicions. An irrational suspicion is why I'm in June's room. A terrible hunch. An intuition. A gnawing fear I need June to dispel. *I know it might sound nuts—*

Cut to the chase, June says, leaning toward the mirror to get her lashes painted right.

I don't know, I say, struggling for words. *Is Grandma Rose really your mother?*

Me, already ashamed, watching June inside the mirror, watching her wide *O* close to a frown, her shaky hand return the clumpy wand to the tube of Maybelline. In the long pause of her silence, I already know I'm right: Grandma Rose isn't her real mother. *And Grandpa Hank?* I say. The best people in our family aren't the family that I thought.

Who told you? June asks, turning to search my face for clues.

No one did. But there's that birth certificate. The missing girl in Great Aunt Ida's family album. The hurried way she closed the book on V. And June without a trace of Grandma Rose's heart. Hank and Rose's great devotion that exceeds what June deserves. What we deserve. *And your real mother, is she V? Grandma Rose's youngest sister?*

Someone had to tell you, June says, angry. *That gossip Ida in Cheyenne. I didn't find out until I was thirty-three years old.*

No one told, I swear. I'm shaking from making this bad hunch true just by saying it aloud. I don't want a missing girl to be June's mother, or June to be a person who began as someone else.

Don't you tell the other kids, June says, one lotioned finger pressed against my lips. *It would break my parents' hearts. They never wanted us to know. And don't you ever tell my parents—*

I won't, I say, eager to protect our beloved Hank and Rose, to be complicit in a secret that will keep us as their own.

V is not our family, never was, June insists, returning to the mirror to finish painting on mascara once her shaky hands have calmed. *Anyway, what difference does it make? None,* she says to her reflection. *Absolutely none.*]

Minor Honor

What Mr. C can offer isn't much—his Ford, some cash, a new bar-boy from Romania Mr. C will pay to get V across the border to Wisconsin. Mr. C can make connections if V still has the goods to sing and dance.

I do, V says. *But us?* Didn't he get her letter? She's eighteen now. They can start over in New York. V can work on Broadway. She can waitress. She'll start at the bottom; she'll find work in a club. She only needs a husband and a job to win June back.

That's quite a tale, kid, he says, interrupting V.

A tale? Don't you love me still? Didn't you promise—

Love? He laughs. *I'm too old for love. I've got a business here to run. Plus—* He gestures toward the band on his left hand. *A year too late,* he says, *but life goes on. I've got my own boy now to raise.* Pale gold in snowy moonlight. Why were they always standing in the snow? *And a wife that won't much like—* He scans the snowy alley on the lookout for police. A nervous habit V remembers well.

And June? V asks. *And June?*

She's all set with your sister. He pats V on the shoulder like a stranger. *Start a clean slate in Wisconsin. You're young enough—*

I'm not, V says, too cold to even cry.

Heaven

1.

Black road in the country, V's driver skids into a ditch to save a deer. Stuck. *Oh shit, oh shit,* the two words he's repeated this entire snowy drive. That and *Mr. C. Oh shit, Mr. C.*

Shut up! V screams. *Mr. C won't help us here.* She spreads the Minnesota map out on her legs, lights a match, finds again that red line border promising Wisconsin. Not much more than an inch. An inch is twenty miles. *I'll walk,* V says. She isn't going to wait for the police. At a farm along this road V will beg for help. A new ride to Milwaukee. *Give your coat to me. Your boots,* V says, pointing at his feet.

No, no. The snow, he says, but V insists.

Across the border, V can make her own way to Chicago, or maybe someplace warmer without this goddamn snow. She can take the train to California to find Em. There isn't any safety sitting here.

What will I tell Mr. C?

Say that you couldn't stop me. Now give me all your money; I'll need every dime.

2.

Wading through the snow, V can't find that state-line border or a house. Can't read the wind-blown map with just the moon. Her tiny size-five feet lost inside the driver's huge galoshes. His heavy coat clearing a path of snow behind her like a trail. A path police could follow if they knew to find V here.

3.

V wakes in a cellar bed of straw and branch, a dirty tarp across her body for a blanket.

I found you on the road, an old man says. White-haired, bearded madman, or maybe God. *Just a little hill of nothing, buried in fresh snow. Brought you to my place to get you warm out of that blizzard. It ain't a palace, but at least you're still alive.*

Alive. V slips her aching hand inside her pocket, feels the roll of cash from Mr. C, the fold of extra bills the driver finally gave her. June's picture she carried from Duluth. Her head pounds from the pain; her legs and feet are numb. But here she is alive.

Did I make it to Wisconsin? Voice nearly gone, her throat tight like a fist. Bones so sore they must be broken.

You did, he nods. *You made it near-dead to Wisconsin. But how much could Wisconsin matter to you, girl?*

Outside, the January day grays toward evening. The library is closing; June's files aren't June's files anymore. Her story in state custody again, one story among the thousands sealed for a century.

I could have gone my whole life without knowing, June says, slipping her arms into her jacket, waiting like a child while I free her zipper from a snag, raise it to her chin, lift the fake fur hood over her curls.

Meaning what? I ask, although I can see June is exhausted. Ready to be done.

Just that, June says. *Exactly what I said.*

She passes me her worn folder full of papers: correspondence with the court and the adoption agency, V's death certificate, her birth certificate, stories she's clipped out of the paper, today's copied file pages we requested from the clerk. State reports, miscellaneous statistics, excerpts from that ledger I won't look at for another fifteen years. *You keep all this,* June tells me, as if this is my inheritance—not cherished heirloom crystal, but this secret we've been sharing since I was twelve years old. This single thing we did together. *You're going to need them for your book.*

What book? I ask, trying to pass them back to June, but she's busy now with leather gloves and can't be bothered.

The one you're going to write, you mark my words.

But we don't even know the story, I say. Every fact we've found today just leads to questions.

We know enough, June says. *Who else is going to tell it?*

June already heading toward the exit, June leaving me to trail her the way I always will.

"I may be mercenary, but I hate poverty, and don't mean to bear it a minute longer than I can help."

— *Amy March, from Louisa May Alcott,* Little Women, *1869*

Exile

V disappears among the exiles in Chicago. A fugitive. A nobody. A nothing. When people ask V who she is, she has a thousand stories she can tell. Reinvention. The fiction of V's life. She's the daughter of a doctor from Detroit. She's a farm girl from Wisconsin. Iowa. Crowned the Dairy Princess in Sioux City three years in a row. She's Val, or Vy, or Vonnie, just like June is Margaret now. Just like Rose was never married in Milwaukee. When V gets a rare audition, she gives her stage name, Venus. Auditions only, because no one in Chicago will hire ordinary V to sing and dance. In a city full of dolls, V's a minor Midwest talent. And what about those stretch marks on her skin? Those spent breasts a baby emptied? *What guy would pay to see that in a show?*

Nights, V works as a dice girl off of Halsted, a flirty 26 Girl, paid to keep the score, to hustle drinks and lure men to the game. *You look like you could use a good strong whiskey. Want in on some action? Wouldn't you like a lucky rabbit's foot tonight?* V, downing gift-drink after gift-drink, Coca-Cola laced with vodka—weak, but still she feels the fog. After close, V becomes the work crew's private showgirl, Baby Vixen. V performing *a capella* the way she used to do with Em.

Walking home alone through darkness, her skin a layer of summer heat and stains strange men have left, V doesn't need a map to know the borders of her life. Her furnished cheap hotel room. The corner store where she buys her Spam and bread. An apple every other day so she stays strong. Far beyond her small asylum: Minneapolis, a place she'll never see again. Dark-eyed June, the daughter V can't hold. The daughter who didn't recognize her mother. V's sisters, the March girls reinvented minus V. V's mother, still living with that man. Mr. C with V's girl heart in the pocket of his vest.

All that V has loved and lost, in a city she can't visit. V in Minneapolis, nevermore.

[How to end a story
that will not end in this life,
or the next, or the next,
because it cannot end?

Generation after generation,
we are walking through V's snow.]

"No girl leaves our home school without a higher ideal, an ideal that in the inevitable, natural force of things must somewhere, somehow, some time find expression. A denial of this would be a denial of the eternal."

—*Fannie French Morse, First Superintendent, Minnesota Home School for Girls at Sauk Centre. Excerpted from* Proceedings of the First State Conference of Child Welfare Boards with The Board of Control, State Capitol, May 9 and 10, 1919, *St. Paul, Minnesota, 1919*

First the Facts, Then the Consequences of the Facts

From the Franklin Bridge into the roiling Mississippi

From the Foshay Tower

From the window of the Met

From the tenth floor of the Nicollet Hotel

From the Wrigley Building

From the Empire State Building

From the Brooklyn Bridge

From the Golden Gate

From the Woolworth Building

From the Chrysler Building

From a balcony off Broadway like so many falling stars

From a hotel window in Hollywood, Chicago, or Detroit

From an ordinary overpass in Champaign, Illinois

V leaps into the air with just her purse—

a spectacle, a comet,

a front-page story in the paper.

V leaps, so she will not die unknown.

"dazzling Venus of the cabarets

　　　and in an instant it is done

　　　　　flashing through the still night

like a comet

　　　the marquee far below

what was once a form

　　　　　to inspire poets

　　　blood

　　　　　　　and shattered bones."

　—*"Beautiful Delores Multiple Heartbreak Ended in a Broadway Tragedy,"*
　　　　　Minneapolis Tribune, *February 16, 1936*

[CODA: 2018

V dead. June lost to dementia. June's children dead now or es-
tranged. Medicated. Adjudicated. Committed on occasion in the
legacy of V. My family that once was, reduced to ruin. *But, V is
not our family, never was.* I drive back to the last place V and June
were family. Minnesota Home School at Sauk Centre, Fairview
Colony for the pregnant and the dim, that cluster of five cottages
where V and June first lived. The trapped girls land-banked on
three sides: jack pine walls around the border, fields rising into
hills, a too steep cliff that cuts into the lake. The old cottage
sweltering in summer, freezing in the winter. Rooms so cold the
inmates shivered in their beds. Bedroom light switch in the hallway so the matron could control V's day and night. A house of
locks and keys. The small tub where V once soaked her swollen
body, felt the animal of June nudge against her ribs. I've come to
see this cottage with the dream that I'll find some evidence of V.
A crazy secret faith: I'll glimpse the ghost of the two of them together, V alive, June a tiny infant in her arms. I want to tell them
how it turns out for our family, the force of things that Fannie
French Morse predicted. That I have done my best to find them,
sealed and erased. Dead or dying. Memory or not. I have tried to
tell their story, the story of us all.]

[*And whose was I?* June asks me now, through the white space of dementia.

V's, I say. *You were V's girl first.*]

DISTRICT COURT
Fourth Judicial District

IN JUVENILE COURT

IN THE MATTER OF

Delinquent
A. ~~Dependent~~ Child
~~Neglected~~

246

V. Venal vortex villain vacant venereal vivacious vulva and vagina vast varied
very voluminous voluptuous vexing voyage vixen vapid vapor vanish vast
valley vanish vanity vain versatile verdict verge verify vilify verb, to V
or not to V, vial vile vertigo vie vice vibrate vicious violin Victrola
visitation visitor visceral visible (in)visible vivid voiceless vodka
voyager and vulture vulnerable vulgar vowel, no not
a vowel, I am a vowel, volatile volunteer
vexing victim vanish
vacant vacant
V.

FOR EVERY V AND JUNE. UNKNOWN.

Mother and Child at Minnesota Home School for Girls at Sauk Centre

Author's Note

In the winter of 2001, I accompanied my mother to the Gale Family Library at the Minnesota History Center in St. Paul, Minnesota. I was in my early forties, my mother in her mid-sixties. We'd come in search of information regarding her birth and her adoption, information held within the restricted records of the Minnesota Home School for Girls at Sauk Centre. In 1935, my mother had been born at that institution, the unplanned daughter of a talented fifteen-year-old inmate serving a six-year sentence at the school. Under Minnesota law, my mother's adoption records were to be sealed for one hundred years, but that January day we arrived with a letter from the court granting my mother's request for access to her own history. Over the next seven hours, side by side at a large table, we worked our way through intake forms, case notes, and adoption records, as well as institutional reports and ledgers available to the public. Encountering my maternal grandmother's file for the first time, I immediately recognized an institutional bias behind the recorded "facts" of the narratives. From the state's questions regarding sexual practices, partners, diseases, and social deviations, to their subjective description of the modest furnishings in her family's apartment, to their inexplicable list of her Jewish acquaintances, I realized the truth we'd hoped to find wasn't in that file.

We'd come in search of my mother's story—her adoption, her biological parents, her conception, her birth—with the belief that her lost story might help us make sense of a lifetime of shared familial traumas. What we found instead were more mysteries to solve. Her young mother's shocking six-year sentence at fifteen. For what? For pregnancy? My mother housed at the institution as an infant to be breast-fed for three months, then taken from her mother? My maternal grandmother finally paroled at eighteen, but what exactly did parole consist of, and why did she subsequently escape parole? Were these troubling discoveries unique to our family, or were other Minnesota girls also victims of this system? And was it only Minnesota? What characterized an "immoral" or "incorrigible" girl in 1935? What made incorrigibility a crime?

Throughout the next decade, I attempted to answer those early questions with additional research. I studied texts and academic articles on the history of female incarceration, the criminalization of female sexuality, the national practice of incarcerating girls for immorality, or girls merely "in danger of becoming immoral." I pursued my suspicion that many of these girls were likely victims of physical or sexual abuse prior to their commitments, and quickly had that hunch confirmed. I read about the history of case records and the professionalization of social work, the creation of juvenile incarceration facilities across America, the Progressive Era, and the Minnesota law that required unmarried women to breastfeed. I researched Minneapolis' history of antisemitism, particularly virulent during the Depression. I immersed myself in 1930s Minneapolis and the rise of the nightclub culture that followed the end of Prohibition. I walked the Minneapolis streets named in that file, believing somehow this gathering of pieces, this immersion into history, would deliver the story of the lost teenage girl, the story my mother longed for when we first opened her file.

And then, more than ten years after the day we saw my mother's file, I requested a fragile, worn book through interlibrary loan at Hamline University where I am a professor in the Creative Writing Program. That invaluable book, *Handbook of American Institutions for Juvenile*

Delinquents, First Edition, Volume I, West North Central States, 1938—published by the Osborne Association, Inc., an organization committed to working with incarcerated men, women, and children, and the families affected by incarceration—was the first in what was to be a nationwide study of institutions for incarcerated juveniles across the United States. It was there, in their carefully documented report, that I began to understand the harsh realities facing the inmates at the Minnesota Home School for Girls at Sauk Centre during the time of my mother's birth, as well as the troubling experiences of incarcerated girls in reformatories in Iowa, Kansas, Missouri, Nebraska, North Dakota, and South Dakota. Reading and rereading the details of that report, I began to imagine my mother's early infancy, and her young mother's difficult days during those interminable years until parole. I learned of the weeks of isolation she would have endured upon arrival, the initial strip search, the school's attempt to separate each girl from all she'd known. I could envision her initial placement at Fairview Colony, a special cluster of cottages for the pregnant and "feeble-minded," and later, her relocation to the main grounds once her baby girl was taken from the school. I learned about the rigor of their schedules, the expectations for daily labor, the cottage system designed to segregate and separate the girls, the corporal punishments of tubbings, isolation, and slaps. And on nearly every page, there was the emphasis on the successful completion of domestic training expected of each girl. In addition to this book, I was aided by the chapter on the 1930s in *A History of the Minnesota Home School 1911–1976*, a report written by Joan McDonald. Finally, the speech of the first Sauk Centre superintendent, Fannie French Morse (1866–1944)—which I have excerpted on pages 76 and 77—provided invaluable perspective on the ethos of this institution where Minnesota girls were held.

The Minnesota Home School for Girls at Sauk Centre, as well as the other institutions featured in the first Osborne Association report, are representative of an extensive network of girls reformatories that spanned the United States in 1938. The push to create reformatories for adolescent girls was well underway in the early part of the twentieth century. Organized primarily by Progressive Era women to reform a criminal justice system focused on the needs and crimes of men, in part this effort aimed to advance a female-centric, women-administered system designed to rehabilitate and protect adolescent girls. The complex factors, biases, and religious overtones influencing this movement are many, as are the motives of reformers, but when my maternal grandmother entered the justice system in 1935, as one of thousands across America, there were institutions ready to house her and countless other "immoral" girls.

According to, *Juvenile Delinquents in Public Institutions, 1933*, prepared by the U.S. Department of Commerce and the Bureau of the Census, girls as young as six were committed to reform institutions in nearly every state. The primary offenses documented for these girls were "sex offenses; immorality and sex delinquency; in danger of leading immoral life; running away; incorrigibility; delinquency." Although these minor status offenses—acts that would not be prosecuted if committed by an adult—were not considered crimes, they nevertheless resulted in commitments until the age of twenty-one for girls in Minnesota. In some states, committed girls and boys shared an institution; in many others, separate institutions were created for the girls. In the 1930s, many of the institutions were racially segregated, either within a shared institution or existing as separate facilities where girls of color were subjected to racial violence. (For a study that examines the historical treatment of African American girls committed as delinquent in Missouri, see Leroy M. Rowe's "A Grave Injustice: Institutional Terror at the State Industrial Home for Negro Girls and the Paradox of Juvenile Delinquent Reform in Missouri, 1888–1960.") Each institution has its own troubling history, a history that spans much of the twentieth century. While some trends in the field of juvenile justice have changed throughout the decades, as late as 1989, when Sauk Centre closed, it was still in use as a detention facility for girls.

Any ambitious researcher looking for a history of abuse within these institutions will likely find it, but the stories we are missing as a nation are the personal narratives of the thousands of girls held for years within those institutions for nothing more than "immorality" or similar non-criminal offenses, the girls victimized within those institutions and in strangers' homes while on parole. The damage done to those sentenced, silenced girls and their descendants is impossible to quantify. Although many of us may be familiar with the practice of institutionalizing "problem" girls in other countries, including the Magdalene Laundries in Ireland, few of us are aware of what happened in America. Shamed by social stigma, dismissed as "bad girls," released to poor employment prospects, or on the run for years as fugitives, few of these girls made their stories known. Even the esteemed performer Ella Fitzgerald, another young aspiring singer and dancer, did not speak of her time at the New York Training School for Girls in 1933, where she was committed as "ungovernable" and subjected to physical abuse.

Unfortunately, the issues girls confront in the juvenile justice system remain distressingly relevant today. According to "The Sexual Abuse to Prison Pipeline: The Girls' Story," published in 2015 by Rights4girls, Georgetown Law Center on Poverty and Inequality, and the Ms. Foundation, "the leading cause of arrest for girls are minor offenses such as misdemeanors, status offenses, outstanding warrants, and technical violations. And the decision to arrest and detain girls in these cases has been shown often to be based in part on the perception of girls having violated conventional norms and stereotypes of feminine behavior." Additionally, girls within the juvenile justice system include a disproportionate number of girls of color, LGBTQ+, and gender nonconforming youth. And while a significant number of girls within the system have been victimized by violence, mental health treatment within residential detention facilities remains inadequate.

More than eighty years beyond my maternal grandmother's incarceration, girls within our current juvenile justice system continue to be violated by strip searches, seclusion, restraints, lack of body privacy, staff mistreatment, and reported incidents of physical and sexual assault. If we hope for meaningful reform within our juvenile justice system, the stories of incarcerated girls, past and present, as well as their descendants, must be heard.

My decision to write this book as an assemblage of fragmented documents and fiction was based on my realization that the truth of my maternal grandmother and her incarceration can't be fully known. Her story, existing in the white space of her absence, is a mystery that my family and I will occupy forever. The facts, the figures, and the observations of the experts included in this book establish the milieu of her time and place, its morals and injustices. It's a world I entered deeply, both imaginatively and intellectually, in search of a veracity I couldn't trust the alleged facts alone to tell.

This book has been an act of inquiry: a decades-long effort to recover the fifteen-year-old dancer and her daughter, my mother, and to consider the consequences of law and history and the ways in which our past, both known and unknown, informs our present. Perhaps most importantly, I am seeking to fill the void with story, to tell myself a tale that will make sense of what I've lost.

I close this book still listening and learning, waiting to hear the stories of survivors and descendants, to be a part of the future research and conversations I hope this work invites.

Bibliography

WORKS CITED

Alcott, Louisa May. *Little Women*. Roberts Bros., 1869.

"Beautiful Delores Multiple Heartbreak Ended in a Broadway Tragedy." *Minneapolis Tribune*, 16 Feb. 1936.

Bigelow, Maurice A. *Sex-Education: A Series of Lectures Concerning Knowledge of Sex in Its Relation to Human Life*. Macmillan, 1916.

"Broken Homes Main Cause of Child Failure." *St. Cloud Daily Times and Daily Journal-Press*, 4 May 1937.

Cox, William B., and F. Lovell Bixby, editors. *Handbook of American Institutions for Delinquent Juveniles, Vol. 1: West North Central States, 1938*. New York: Osborne Assoc., 1938.

Lundberg, Emma O. *Children of Illegitimate Birth and Measures for Their Protection*. Bureau Publication No. 166. United States, Dept. of Labor, Children's Bureau, Government Printing Office, 1926.

Lunden, Walter A. *Juvenile Delinquency: Manual and Source Book*. U of Pittsburgh, 1936.

Mason's Minnesota Statutes 1927. Compiled and edited by the editorial staff of the Citer-Digest Company, St. Paul, 1927.

1936 Supplement to Mason's Minnesota Statutes, 1927. St. Paul: Citer-Digest Co., 1936.

Milosz, Czeslaw. *Bells in Winter*. Ecco, 1988.

New Webster's Dictionary of the English Language. Encyclopedic Edition with a Library of Useful Knowledge. DeLair, 1980.

Proceedings of the First State Conference of Child Welfare Boards with the Board of Control, State Capitol, May 9 and 10, 1919, St. Paul, Minnesota.

"Report of Population for Month Ending November 30, 1935." Minnesota Home School for Girls at Sauk Centre, Case files, Minnesota Historical Society.

"Report to the Minnesota State Board of Control." June 30, 1936. Minnesota Home School for Girls at Sauk Centre, Case files, Minnesota Historical Society.

"Report to the Minnesota State Board of Control." June 30, 1938. Minnesota Home School for Girls at Sauk Centre, Case files, Minnesota Historical Society.

Sadler, William S., and Lena K. Sadler. *The Mother and Her Child*. Chicago: A. C. McClurg & Co., 1916.

"School Days and Night Life Mix." *Duluth News-Tribune*, 2 Feb. 1939.

Trumbull, Henry Clay. *Teaching and Teachers*. Philadelphia: John D. Wattles, 1884.

United States, Department of Commerce, Bureau of the Census. *Juvenile Delinquents in Public Institutions, 1933*. Government Printing Office, 1936.

ADDITIONAL REFERENCE MATERIALS

BOOKS

Alexander, Ruth M. *"The Girl Problem": Female Sexual Delinquency in New York 1900–1930*. Cornell UP, 1995.

Brenzel, Barbara. *Daughters of the State: A Social Portrait of the First Reform School for Girls in North America, 1856–1905*. MIT P, 1983.

Chatelain, Marcia. *South Side Girls: Growing Up in the Great Migration*. Duke UP, 2015.

Chesney-Lind, Meda, and Randall G. Sheldon. *Girls: Delinquency and Juvenile Justice*. Brooks/Cole, 1992.

Chesney-Lind, Meda, and Lisa Pasko. *The Female Offender: Girls, Women, and Crime*. 2nd ed., Sage, 2004.

Cressey, Paul G. *The Taxi-Dance Hall: A Sociological Study in Commercialized Recreation and City Life*. 1932. U of Chicago P, 2008.

Dodge, L. Mara. *"Whores and Thieves of the Worst Kind": A Study of Women, Crime and Prisons, 1835–2000*. Northern Illinois UP, 2006.

Inness, Sherrie A. *Delinquents and Debutantes: Twentieth-Century American Girls' Cultures*. NYU P, 1998.

Karlen, Neal. *Augie's Secrets: The Minneapolis Mob and the King of the Hennepin Strip*. Minnesota Historical Society P, 2014.

Konopka, Gisela. *The Adolescent Girl in Conflict*. Prentice Hall, 1966.

Kunzel, Regina G. *Fallen Women, Problem Girls: Unmarried Mothers and the Professionalization of Social Work, 1890–1945*. Yale UP, 1995.

Lindenmeyer, Kriste. *The Greatest Generation Grows Up: American Childhood in the 1930s*. Ivan R. Dee, 2005.

McDonald, Joan. *A History of the Minnesota Home School 1911–1976*. Minnesota Home School Citizens Committee, 1976.

Odem, Mary E. *Delinquent Daughters: Protecting and Policing Adolescent Female Sexuality in the United States, 1885–1920*. U of North Carolina P, 1995.

Platt, Anthony M. *The Child Savers: The Invention of Delinquency*. 1969. Rutgers UP, 2009.

Rosheim, David L. *The Other Minneapolis, or A History of the Minneapolis Skid Row*. Andromeda, 1978.

Salerno, Roger A. *Sociology Noir: Studies at the University of Chicago in Loneliness, Marginality and Deviance, 1915–1935.* McFarland & Company, 2007.

Solinger, Rickie. *Wake Up Little Susie: Single Pregnancy and Race Before Roe V. Wade.* Routledge, 1992.

Thomas, William I. *The Unadjusted Girl.* Little Brown, 1923.

Tice, Karen W. *Tales of Wayward Girls and Immoral Women: Case Records and the Professionalization of Social Work.* U of Illinois P, 1998.

Tiffin, Susan. *In Whose Best Interest? Child Welfare Reform in the Progressive Era.* Praeger, 1982.

Zahn, Margaret A., editor. *The Delinquent Girl.* Temple UP, 2009.

REPORTS AND GOVERNMENT DOCUMENTS

Dietzler, Mary Macey. *Detention Houses and Reformatories as Protective Social Agencies in the Campaign of the United States Government Against Venereal Diseases.* The United States Interdepartmental Social Hygiene Board, Government Printing Office, June 1922.

Epstein, Rebecca, Yasmin Vafa, and Rebecca Burney, editors. *I Am the Voice: Girls' Reflections from Inside the Justice System.* Georgetown Law Center on Poverty and Inequality; Rights4Girls, 2018.

Gibson, Campbell, and Kay Jung. United States, Census Bureau, Population Division, Working Paper No. 56. *Historical Census Statistics on Population Totals by Race, 1790 To 1990, and By Hispanic Origin, 1970 to 1990, for the United States, Regions, Divisions, and States.* Government Printing Office, Sept. 2002.

Kerig, Patricia K., and Julian D. Ford. *Trauma Among Girls in the Juvenile Justice System.* National Child Traumatic Stress Network Center for Trauma Recovery and Juvenile Justice, and the Network Juvenile Justice Working Group, 2014.

LaDu, Blanche L. *A Picture of Minnesota in 1932*. Address given at the State Conference of Social Work, Sept. 1932.

Saar, Malika Saada, Rebecca Epstein, Lindsay Rosenthal, and Yasmin Vafa. *The Sexual Abuse to Prison Pipeline: The Girls' Story*. Human Rights Projects for Girls, Georgetown Law Center on Poverty and Inequality, Ms. Foundation for Women, 2015.

Sherman, Francine T., and Annie Balck. *Gender Injustice: System-Level Juvenile Justice Reforms for Girls*. The National Crittenton Foundation, and National Women's Law Center, 2015.

State of Minnesota, Office of the Legislative Auditor, Program Evaluation Division. *Residential Facilities for Juvenile Offenders*. Feb. 1995.

Swayze, Dana Hurley, and Danette Buskovick. *Youth in Minnesota Correctional Facilities: Responses to the 2013 Minnesota Student Survey*. Minnesota Department of Public Safety Office of Justice Programs, Oct. 2014.

Weber, Laura E. *"Gentiles Preferred": Minneapolis Jews and Employment, 1920–1950*. Minnesota Historical Society, Spring 1991.

MEDIA

Bernstein, Nina. "Ward of the State: The Gap in Ella Fitzgerald's Life." *The New York Times*, 23 June 1996, p. D4.

Brown, Curt. "Anti-Semitism Flared in Minnesota Long Ago." *Star Tribune*, 18 Mar. 2017, http://www.startribune.com/anti-semitism-flared-in-minnesota-long-ago/416516923.

Franklin, Robert. "A Hard Look Back at the Old Home School." *Star Tribune*, 13 Jan. 2002, p. 9B.

Franklin, Robert. "New Vision for Sauk Centre's Old Reform School: Owners Think Campus Ideal for College or Business." *Star Tribune*, 13 Jan. 2002, p. 1B.

Hollingsworth, Heather. "Girls Reformatory Leaves Legacy of Hurt, Haven." *NBC News*, 24 Oct. 2009, http://www.nbcnews.com/id/33461470/ns/us_news-life/t/girls-reformatory-leaves-legacy-hurt-haven.

Khazan, Olga. "Inherited Trauma Shapes Your Health." *The Atlantic*, 16 Oct. 2018, https://www.theatlantic.com/health/archive/2018/10/trauma-inherited-generations/573055.

Maccabee, Paul. "Alias Kid Cann." *Mpls. St. Paul*, vol. 19, no. 11, Nov. 1991, pp. 88-91.

Serres, Chris. "Jailed, Abused for No Crime." *Star Tribune*, 7 Aug. 2016, p. 1A.

We Knew Who We Were: Memories of the Minneapolis Jewish North Side. Directed by Thomas F. Lieberman, The Jewish Historical Society of the Upper Midwest and The North Side Committee, 2008.

Yager, Sarah. "Prison Born." *The Atlantic*, July/Aug. 2015, https://www.theatlantic.com/magazine/archive/2015/07/prison-born/395297.

Zollman, Bryan. "Abandoned Souls? Questions Linger About History of Brookdale Cemetery." *Sauk Centre Herald*, 19 June 2013.

JOURNAL ARTICLES, DISSERTATIONS, AND THESES

Kinzelman, Cara Armida. *A Certain Kind of Girl: Social Workers and the Creation of the Pathological Unwed Mother, 1918–1940.* 2013. U of Minnesota, PhD dissertation.

Kremer, Gary R., and Linda Rea Gibbens. "The Missouri Home for Negro Girls: The 1930s." *American Studies*, vol. 24, no. 2, 1983, pp. 77–93. *JSTOR*, www.jstor.org/stable/40641775.

Leavitt, Sarah A. *Neglected, Vagrant, and Viciously Inclined: The Girls of the Connecticut Industrial School, 1867–1917.* 1992. Wesleyan U, BA

thesis. https://wesscholar.wesleyan.edu/cgi/viewcontent.cgi?article=
1388&context=etd_hon_theses.

Myers, Tamara, and Joan Sangster. "Retorts, Runaways and Riots: Pat-
terns of Resistance in Canadian Reform Schools for Girls, 1930–60."
Journal of Social History, vol. 34, no. 3, Spring 2001, pp. 669–697.
EBSCOhost, doi:10.1353/jsh.2001.0025.

Pasko, Lisa. "Damaged Daughters: The History of Girls' Sexuality and
the Juvenile Justice System." *Journal of Criminal Law & Criminology*,
vol. 100, no. 3, Summer 2010, pp. 1099–1130. *JSTOR*, www.jstor.
org/stable/25766116.

Rosenthal, Marguerite G. "Reforming the Juvenile Correctional Institution: Efforts of the U.S. Children's Bureau in the 1930s." *Journal of
Sociology and Social Welfare*, vol. 14, no. 4, Dec. 1987, pp. 47–74.

Rowe, Leroy M. "A Grave Injustice: Institutional Terror at the State Industrial Home for Negro Girls and the Paradox of Juvenile Delinquent Reform in Missouri, 1888–1960." 2006. U of Missouri, Co-
lumbia, MA Thesis.

Tannenbaum, Nili, and Michael Reisch. "From Charitable Volunteers to
Architects of Social Welfare: A Brief History of Social Work." *Ongoing
Magazine*, U of Michigan School of Social Work, Fall 2001, pp. 6–11,
https://ssw.umich.edu/about/history/brief-history-of-social-work.

ARCHIVAL COLLECTIONS

Minnesota Historical Society

Prison Memory Project

Sauk Centre History Museum and Research Center

Stearns History Museum

Permissions

Page 78, "Morse Hall." Used with permission of Stearns County History Museum.

Page 97, "A Group of Girls Outside Pioneer Cottage." Used with permission of Stearns History Museum.

Page 102, "Mother Daughter Puzzle." Photograph by Bob Armstrong. Wooden puzzle circa 1909. Restored by and in the collection of Bob Armstrong and displayed at: www.oldpuzzles.com. Used with permission of Bob Armstrong.

Page 138, "Babies at Minnesota Home School for Girls at Sauk Centre." Used with permission of the Sauk Centre History Museum and Research Center.

Page 146, "View at Home School for Girls Sauk Centre, Minnesota." Used with permission of Minnesota Historical Society.

Page 160, "Girls Working in the Field." Used with permission of Stearns History Museum.

Page 243, Lines from "Beautiful Delores Multiple Heartbreak Ended in a Broadway Tragedy," *Minneapolis Tribune*, February 16, 1936. Usage licensed by the Associated Press: Copyrighted 1936. Associated Press. 279279:0619PF.

Page 249, "Mother and Child at Minnesota Home School for Girls at Sauk Centre." Used with permission of Sauk Centre History Museum and Research Center.

Acknowledgments

It's a daunting task to thank all who have made this work possible over the past decade.

First and most importantly, thank you to my daughter, Mikaela, who believed in this book from the beginning and waited every day to hear the words I wrote. First listener. First believer. This book belongs to you. Thank you to my son, Dylan, for countless conversations on art and life and V. Thank you to my husband, Tim, true champion of my every book—thirty years and six books later, I'm grateful you're still here. Gratitude to Martin Case, loyal friend and fellow writer; to Kate Shuknecht and Lacey Buchda, my first-rate editorial assistants; and to my generous early readers: Maureen Gibbon, Rachel Moritz, Josie Sigler Sibara, Callie Cardamon, Susan Wolter Nettell, Meghan Maloney-Vinz, and Nico Taranovsky. To all my friends who have listened and urged me forward, thank you. You know who you are; you have my heart.

A huge debt is owed to the Osborne Association who set out across America in 1937 to document juvenile detention facilities and whose reports made the veracity of V's story possible. Their contributions to America's knowledge of juvenile detention facilities at the time is immeasurable, as are their contributions to this book. More than eighty years beyond that first report, they are still working for justice. Thank you to Joan McDonald for her report, *A History of the Minnesota Home School 1911–1976* published by the Minnesota Home School Citizens Committee, and to Cara Armida Kinzelman for her dissertation, *A Cer-*

tain *Kind of Girl: Social Workers and the Creation of the Pathological Unwed Mother, 1918–1940*. Thank you to Sharon Sandeen, Ben Welter, and James Shiffer for answering my many questions. And to all the writers, scholars, and activists, past and present, committed to justice for incarcerated girls, I thank you.

My appreciation to the Sauk Centre Historical Museum and Research Center, and the people of Sauk Centre who have been especially helpful: Matt and Erin Bjork, Pam Borgmann, and former staff from the school who shared poems and stories of the girls. A special thank you to Eagle's Healing Nest for transforming the former Minnesota Home School for Girls into a place committed to healing the invisible wounds of war for veterans, and to Chair/Director Melony Butler, for granting us permission to both visit and film the grounds. For research support at Hamline University, thank you to librarians Siobhan Dizio and Amy Sheehan.

Thank you to Robert Hedin for making possible the work of so many artists and writers, and to The Anderson Center at Tower View for giving me uninterrupted writing time and space to bring this book to completion. I am also grateful to the Studium at the College of St. Benedict for the silent days to work. Immense gratitude to Minnesota State Arts Board for not one, but two Artist Initiative grants to bring this story into the world despite real obstacles, and for believing with me that this history of Minnesota girls should matter to us all. Without their support, this book would still be a dream. Thank you to Andrea Smith, extraordinary librarian at the Minnesota Correctional Facility-Shakopee, for the opportunities to share my work, and thank you to the women there for the work they've shared with me. A note of thanks to historian Bill Millikan, for telling me all those years ago where my mother's records could be found, and to the Minnesota Historical Society for holding the archives from the Minnesota Home School for Girls at Sauk Centre. A huge thank you to Abigail

Beckel and Kathleen Rooney, my brilliant, ambitious editors at Rose Metal Press for their deep commitment to writing that exists outside the boundaries and for their careful attention to craft; I'm proud to be among their writers.

Most significantly, I am indebted to my mother for her indomitable spirit, her remarkable refusal to conform, and for raising me to both see, and speak against, the oppression of girls and women, and to fight for gender justice. Thank you to my beloved grandparents, Howard and Dorothy, for giving us a home and family, and for providing a model of infinite, unconditional love. And to that talented young girl who brought my mother into being, for that sacrifice and so much more, I thank you now.

About the Author

Sheila O'Connor is the author of six award-winning novels for adults and young people. Her books include *Where No Gods Came*, winner of the Minnesota Book Award and the Michigan Prize for Literary Fiction, and *Sparrow Road*, winner of the International Reading Award. Her novels have been included on Best Books of the Year lists by *Booklist*, *VOYA*, *Book Page*, and the Chicago Public Library, among others. O'Connor received her MFA in Poetry from the University of Iowa Writers' Workshop, and her work across genres has been recognized with the Loft Literary Center's McKnight Fellowship, two Bush Artist Fellowships, and several Artist Initiative grants from the Minnesota State Arts Board. She is a professor in the Creative Writing Programs at Hamline University in St. Paul, Minnesota, where she serves as fiction editor for *Water~Stone Review*. Learn more at www.sheilaoconnor.com.

A Note about the Type

Evidence of V begins in the 1930s and delves into a dark chapter of American history, rendering family events and criminal justice system issues with consequences that reverberate into the present. Fonts were chosen with respect for the weight of the story, and to match Sheila O'Connor's weaving of the past and present.

The body text is set in Berkeley Old Style, which was designed by Frederic Goudy in 1938—the period of time in which V was alive—and Tony Stan redrew the font family in 1983. It features lovely light calligraphic details, and was designed to be highly legible at small sizes, making it ideal for book interiors.

The display font used throughout the interior and on the cover is Questa Sans, a sans serif family published in 2014 by the Questa Project —a collaboration between designers Martin Majoor and Jos Buivenga. It was designed in the warm, humanistic style of the original grotesque fonts popularized in the early 1900s and used heavily in posters and marquees of the Depression Era.

Special Elite is a vintage typewriter–style font used for the historical file text in the interior, and also for the title on the cover. It was chosen to reflect the look of typewriter lettering prevalent during the time V's case file would have been written. It was designed by Brian J. Bonislawsky of the Astigmatic One Eye Typographic Institute in 2011.

—Heather Butterfield